Dial Books for Young Readers
An imprint of Penguin Random House LLC, New York

First published in the United States of America by Dial Books for Young Readers,
an imprint of Penguin Random House LLC, 2021

Visit us online at penguinrandomhouse.com.

Library of Congress Cataloging-in-Publication Data is available.
Printed in the United States of America
ISBN 9780593112298

10 9 8 7 6 5 4 3 2 1

Design by Mina Chung
Text set in Neutraface Slab

The MANY MYSTERIES of the FINKEL FAMILY

SARAH KAPIT

DIAL BOOKS FOR YOUNG READERS

For Neil

CHAPTER ONE:

IN WHICH A NEW BUSINESS IS FOUNDED

DO YOU HAVE A MYSTERY THAT NEEDS SOLVING?

Finkel Investigation Agency Solving Consequential
Crimes Only (FIASCCO) is here to help!

Our team of experienced detectives can solve all/most
mysteries, including theft, missing pets, and other matters
requiring detecting skill and general awesomeness.

For more information, talk to Lara Finkel ASAP.

NOTE: FIASCCO cannot help find murderers. If you or someone
you know has been murdered, please call a grown-up.

Lara looked over her flyer with a great big frown. It really was too bad she couldn't come up with a name that spelled out FIASCO instead of FIASCCO. She was an excellent speller, in addition to being an excellent investigator. She didn't want anyone to get the wrong idea about that. But it was too late now to change the name. Her parents had not been pleased with her printing so many copies of her flyer using the family printer, and they'd clearly stated that there would be no second edition. So Lara would just have to live with FIASCCO.

Her mother had also insisted that Lara add in the part about not solving murders. At first she'd resisted. After all, Georgia Ketteridge, Girl Super-Detective, would never turn down a murder case if she were lucky enough to find one. But given Lara's unfortunate tendency to get nauseous whenever she saw even a drop of blood, maybe Ima had a point.

Okay, so Lara wouldn't be solving murder cases straight off. So what? She felt completely, totally, 100 percent certain that detective work was going to be her thing. Her cousin Aviva had math, and her sister, Caroline, had art, and her brother Benny had science-y things. Now, Lara would have detecting. Which just so happened to be way cooler than any of those other things. After having read all four books in the Georgia Ketteridge series, Lara knew she could solve a real-life mystery. If only one would come to her.

It'll come, Lara told herself. The flyers were just step one.

With her mission in mind, Lara gathered up the stack of flyers and headed for the door. It was still only the early afternoon, leaving plenty of time to redecorate the neighborhood in blazing-yellow flyers—not Lara's favorite color, but good for getting attention. Hopefully.

For a moment Lara considered enlisting Caroline's help in the matter. As annoying as her little sister could be—very!—Caroline usually made things more fun. She should get Caroline. Yet something inside her rebelled at the idea. Maybe Caroline was her very favorite sibling, separated by a mere fifteen months, but did that mean they had to do absolutely everything together?

No, Lara decided. It did not.

Lara paused when she reached the kitchen. Based on the too-loud talk and enticing vanilla scent, she deduced two things. First, her sister and cousin were in there. Second, they were baking cupcakes. Without her.

Stupid show-off Aviva and her stupid show-off cupcakes. As if it weren't enough that her cousin moved in last year and immediately became the smartest kid in Lara's grade. Apparently, she also had to bake cupcakes several times a week. They were good cupcakes, too. Lara supposed that was one reason why her sister and brothers failed to recognize the fact that Aviva was actually annoying.

Lara couldn't help it. She marched into the kitchen.

"Hello, Lara," her cousin said, not looking up from her mixing bowl. "We've already put the cupcakes in the oven. But you can still decorate them with us if you want."

"Pretty please? It will be fun," Caroline said. She spoke

using a computer voice that came out of her tablet. That was how Caroline talked. She'd type things into an app, and then a voice from her tablet—a snotty-sounding British lady—would speak her words out loud.

"No," Lara said firmly. Detective business required her full attention.

She was about to leave Caroline and Aviva for good when her older brother, Noah, walked in.

"Hello annoying sisters," he said. "And not-at-all annoying cousin who makes excellent baked goods."

Lara stuck her tongue out at him and straightened her stack of flyers.

"I helped with the cupcakes. Do you want to reconsider?"

"In that case, I take it back until I've got my cupcakes. At least for you, Lina-Lin." Noah gave his cheekiest smile. His eyes fell on Lara's stack of flyers. "Huh. What do you have there, Lara?"

Noah snatched a flyer without asking. As he read, Lara twirled a piece of hair. It's not like she needed Noah's permission for anything. Of course she didn't. Still, she cared what her brother thought. A lot.

"Um. How are you an experienced detective?" Noah asked.

Lara scowled. Rude!

"I found Benny's favorite toy car for him last week, after everyone else gave up on it," she informed her brother. "Plus I figured out the cause of Kugel's hairball problem. It was the kettle corn he kept sneaking in the middle of the night."

"So you're going from hairball investigations to solving actual mysteries?"

A snicker came from Aviva's corner of the room. Lara forced herself to stay focused. Aviva's opinions did not matter in the slightest.

"Absolutely," Lara said. "The Mystery of the Hairball was very difficult to crack. And now Kugel hasn't had a single hairball in two weeks thanks to me."

"That is a true miracle."

"Yes, it is," Lara said, nobly choosing to ignore Noah's sarcasm.

Fists clenched, Lara reminded herself that Georgia Ketteridge was graceful even when dealing with annoying people.

"Why are you calling it *F-I-A-S-C-C-O*?" he asked.

"Because it sounds good. Any new business needs a marketing plan."

"Sure," Noah said in his I'm-going-to-tell-you-what-you-want-to-hear-but-I-don't-really-mean-it voice. Lara despised that voice. "Um, you do know what *fiasco* means, right?"

Lara snatched the flyer out of Noah's hands. "Of course I do."

"Then why did you name your detective agency after it?"

"Well, the idea is that when you have a fiasco, you go to FIASCCO. Get it?"

"Not really," Noah muttered.

"It does not make sense to me, either," Aviva said. As if anyone had asked her!

That was quite enough. Noah and Aviva just didn't understand. Unfortunate, certainly, but it's not like Lara actually needed help from them. Or anyone else. She straightened her pile of flyers and gave everyone a properly disdainful look. Well, at least she hoped it showed proper disdain.

"I am going to post these around. If anyone you know needs mystery-solving services, I'm here to help," she said.

And she marched out of the house clutching her flyers.

It took more than an hour, but every house on the block got a FIASCCO flyer. With every paper she placed on a doorstep, hope swelled in Lara's chest. True, she didn't know if anyone on the street needed a detective. But surely someone out of all these people would want to hire her.

As she went from door to door, Lara allowed her mind to wander. She had heard—many, many times—that people on the autism spectrum were blessed with extraordinary abilities. But she couldn't help but think that somehow this particular trait had passed her by.

Once, she'd said as much to Ima, who responded with a sigh. "You're a fast reader," her mother pointed out. "And you remember what you read perfectly."

"Only because I read my books so many times!"

Lara loved books as though they were dear friends. In her experience, they were certainly more reliable than people-friends. But honestly, what kind of a special talent was *reading*? Ima didn't get it at all.

"And you're good at writing, too," Ima had continued. "All of your teachers praise your essays."

There wasn't much point in saying that writing essays was a rather unimpressive talent. Ima would only protest. Even though it was totally and completely true.

After all, Lara reasoned, they didn't put essays up next to the great paintings in museums. Nobody had ever written a newspaper article about a particularly skilled essay-writer. Kids at school never told her "Great essay! Can you show me how to do that?" the way people did with Caroline's drawings.

Detective work was different. Once she succeeded with that, she would be special too.

For a moment, Lara wondered if flyers were perhaps not the preferred method for finding mysteries. In the Georgia Ketteridge books, mysteries just appeared. Georgia's uncle once fell victim to an attempted robbery. But Lara couldn't count on that kind of luck.

As she marched back to her house, Lara's mind burst with thoughts of her detective agency. She felt confident— well, mostly confident—that she could find a mystery before school started up again in a few weeks. After that, maybe there would be school-related mysteries for her to solve. And then? Why, she'd practically be an established detective.

She even had her very own detective notebook. True, it was just a black-and-white composition notebook that said "FIASCCO" on the front, but still. It counted.

"What are you doing?" a voice asked.

Lara spun around to find Caroline, who was wearing her special harness and straps. It helped her lug around her tablet without tiring out her arms too much.

Caroline's computer voice always spoke in the same flat tone. Still, Lara could swear that her sister sounded extra whiny.

"Oh, I was just delivering flyers for my new detective agency," Lara said. Her chest swelled at the word *my*.

"Can I help?"

"No!" Lara said immediately. The look on Caroline's face made her stomach squirm. "I mean, I'm almost done. So you can't. Sorry."

That ought to do it, she thought. Caroline couldn't possibly stay upset for long. Right?

"Why didn't you ask me to help?" her sister asked. After she finished typing she looked expectantly at Lara.

Lara knew she should make up some excuse about having forgotten to ask. Caroline would believe her. Probably. But when she opened her mouth to invent something that sounded believable, entirely different words came out. "I didn't need your help."

Big mistake. Caroline tapped away at her tablet, her jaw clenched firmly. Lara bounced on her toes while she waited for her sister to finish typing.

"I would be good at being a detective," Caroline said finally. "I would."

Lara blinked. She had not considered whether or not

her sister would be good at detecting. That wasn't the point. The whole point of FIASCCO was that she, Lara Finkel, was going to be a detective. Caroline already had her special thing!

Gulping in a deep breath, Lara prepared herself to say something wise and sisterly. Something that would magically make Caroline understand why she absolutely could not be a part of FIASCCO.

Instead, Lara said, "Are you absolutely sure about that? There's a lot that goes into being a detective, you know."

The moment the words escaped her mouth Lara realized her mistake. Caroline tore her eyes away from the screen and delivered a glare that made Lara's ankles shake. It really was remarkable how her eleven-year-old sister could imitate their mother so precisely.

"Just because I can't talk doesn't mean that I can't be a detective, Lara."

As always, Caroline's computer voice did not waver. She might as well have been reciting state capitals. Or commenting on the rather large number of trees in Seattle. But Lara knew her sister was capital-*U* Upset. She knew it from the tightness of Caroline's jaw and the clenched fist flapping by her side.

"I never said you can't be a detective." Lara did her best

to imitate the tablet's calm monotone, but a squeak crept into her voice. "I just said you couldn't be in FIASCCO."

Logically, Lara knew that such a distinction was unlikely to satisfy her sister. Yet it was true. If Caroline couldn't see that, it wasn't Lara's problem.

Caroline glared at Lara's last remaining flyer as though it reeked of Kugel's litter box contents. Her fingers danced across the screen at top speed, and Lara didn't have to wait very long at all to hear her response.

"Fine. Be that way. By the way, 'fiasco' is a stupid name."

And with that, Caroline closed her tablet shut and marched back toward the house. As Lara watched Caroline disappear behind the bright yellow door, she chewed on the edges of her lip.

For a moment, Lara considered going after her sister and begging for forgiveness. She made it three whole steps before drawing to a stop.

Lara wasn't going to apologize for starting her own detective agency. After all, it wasn't like Caroline did absolutely everything with her. Lara thought of the many occasions when she'd walked in on her sister doing something with Aviva. Like baking cupcakes, for example. Caroline hadn't apologized to Lara for the fact that she apparently preferred to spend time in the company of the world's most annoying cousin. Why should Lara apologize for FIASCCO?

Feeling satisfied with her decision to not apologize for anything, Lara posted the final FIASCCO flyer on a large tree in the Finkels' front yard.

Just as she was admiring her work, her father very rudely interrupted. From his place in his parked car, he tapped up against the car window. Lara jumped. "Lara-bear!" he said. "Get in the car. I need you and your sister for some things."

"What things?" she asked crossly.

"Consider it adventuring of the errands variety," Dad replied.

That was not promising. Lara groaned, but she marched over and got into her father's car. When she glanced out the window and spotted her flyer, she couldn't help but smile. FIASCCO would succeed. She felt sure of it.

A moment later, Caroline entered the car. She did not say anything to Lara. She didn't even bother keeping her speech app open, but instead started playing Candy Crush.

Fine. It's not like Lara actually needed her sister.

CHAPTER TWO:

SUMMER SCHOOL DAYS

When Dad told her they were going on an adventure of the errands variety, Caroline had hoped it might be at least vaguely interesting. And it was. The problem was that it was the wrong kind of interesting.

"We're going to school and meeting with Principal Jenkins," Dad told them as he pulled the car out of the driveway.

At that news Lara crossed her arms across her chest. "We can't possibly be in trouble yet! School hasn't even started."

Even though she agreed with her sister, Caroline did not say anything. She was still supposed to be mad at Lara, after all.

"You're not in trouble. This is just a visit," Dad said.

"Aren't we going to spend enough time there once school starts?" Lara asked.

Dad smiled, but it looked a bit strained. "My signature is needed on some paperwork. I've been so busy with work that I forgot to mail some things in. Luckily the school is being understanding."

Of course. Her father was good at many things, but paperwork was not one of them. It probably had to do with the fact that he had ADHD. As an investigative journalist he was brilliant at figuring out powerful people's secrets, yet somehow filling out a two-page form on time eluded him. That was just Dad.

"Anyway," Dad continued. "Since I'll be going in for the bureaucratic stuff, the principal and I thought it would be a good idea for Lina-Lin to see the school before she begins." He looked at Caroline in the rearview. "We want you to feel right at home from your very first day."

The words made Caroline bounce around in her seat. In just a week, she would go to middle school for the first time ever. The prospect filled her with excitement—and, okay, maybe just a little bit of terror.

Her six years of elementary school had left much to be desired. For her first few years Caroline had been in special education—an experience she would gladly scrub completely from her memory were it possible to do so. In special ed., teachers talked in weird voices and made Caroline read books that were way too easy for her. They had lessons like "How to Make a Bed," as if Ima hadn't taught her how to do that when she was five. When the school finally decided she could move to regular classes, Caroline had cheered. Silently, of course.

Even then, a paraprofessional had shadowed her every move. Sometimes that was helpful, like when things got too loud, too bright, too everything. Still, Caroline would have preferred not to have the help. Not many kids invited the autistic girl with a speech device and paraprofessional to play tag with them during recess.

Middle school was going to be different. After much talk and pleading on Caroline's part, it was decided that she could be on her own. There would be no paraprofessional hovering, offering help and high fives and bad jokes. She, Caroline Finkel, would be in charge.

And maybe, just maybe . . . she could be more than just the girl who didn't talk in the normal way.

It was all very exciting, if more than a little terrifying. Visiting ahead of time was a good idea. New places tended to make Caroline nervous. Still, she couldn't help but wonder if normal kids—the ones who spoke with their mouths—visited school the week before it began. She suspected not.

"Exactly what am I supposed to do while we're there?"

Lara asked. Obviously she was still cross about who-even-knows-what. "I know where everything is already."

"Exactamundo, Lara-bear. I was hoping you could give your sister a tour. You know, show her all of the cool hangouts. I'm sure you know much more about that than us old people," Dad said.

"Dad, no one calls places 'hangouts.'"

"See? You're already proving my point."

Caroline glanced at her sister. Maybe a tour would help them fix their sort-of fight.

"I would like you to give me a tour, Lara," she typed.

Lara gave her a small smile. "I guess I can do that."

And so Caroline soon found herself in Principal Jenkins's office, listening to the small blond woman ramble on about how Pinecone Arts Academy was an inclusive environment. Caroline wondered why it was necessary to repeat this statement seven times in fifteen minutes, but did not say so out loud.

Luckily, Dad saved her from being subjected to more boring talk.

"Caroline's sister is outside," he said. "I was hoping that Lara could give her a tour of the school."

"Oh yes, of course!" Principal Jenkins said. "Please do take a look around. And don't be a stranger! I know you won't be getting in trouble and ending up here, but I'd love to shoot the breeze with you sometime."

Caroline agreed, although she had little desire to chat—or shoot the breeze or whatever you called it—with Principal Jenkins.

And why was the principal so sure that Caroline wouldn't get into trouble? She frowned. Perhaps it was silly, but now she almost wanted to prove Principal Jenkins wrong and do something just a little bit naughty. Caroline filed the thought away for further consideration. Right now, she needed to focus on learning how to get around this place by herself.

"Finally," Lara said when she saw Caroline. Her irritation appeared to have faded, much to Caroline's relief. "What were you doing in there, anyway?"

"Boring stuff. Now are you going to show me all of the cool places around here?"

Lara rolled her eyes. "There are no cool places around here, and even if there were, I certainly wouldn't know them. But I can show you all the big things. Where do you want to begin?"

There were lots of places Caroline wanted to see, especially the art rooms. Pinecone Arts Academy was known for its arts programs, as Dad and Ima mentioned approximately eight million times over the past week. And art, after all, was her thing. But that's not what she asked to see first. "What's your favorite place?" she asked her sister.

"Here?"

"Yes."

"I really haven't thought about that," Lara admitted. "I don't exactly consider school one of my favorite places at all."

"There has to be a place here that you think is less bad than the other places," Caroline pressed.

For several moments Lara didn't say anything else. But she soon took off at a brisk walk, forcing Caroline to take large strides to keep up.

If Caroline had been forced to guess her sister's favorite place at school, she probably would have selected the library. But that wasn't it at all. Lara led her through several series of doorways before reaching a courtyard. Once there, she marched right up to a scraggly old tree along the courtyard's edge.

"This is my tree," Lara said.

"It's a nice tree," Caroline told her, even though there wasn't really anything special about it. "Why do you like it?"

Stroking the bark, Lara chewed on her lip. "It's . . . it's just a good place to come and think. When I want quiet, you know. Especially when it rains. That's the best time to come out here."

Caroline had never known her sister to have a particular fondness for trees. But she could picture Lara coming out to the courtyard to be alone. There was something very comforting about that picture.

"When I'm at school, can I come here too?" she asked.

Something flashed across Lara's face, and Caroline regretted asking the question.

"I like to be alone here," Lara said.

"Okay."

It was, Caroline supposed, only fair. But when she thought about going to school—in a week!—and facing all of the students and teachers and their noise, she couldn't help but get antsy. No wonder Lara came here for quiet.

"If I really, really needed it, could I come?" Caroline said, hesitating only slightly.

"If you really, really need it, then it's your tree."

Caroline beamed. She probably wouldn't come to her sister's tree. But knowing that it was here for her made her feel just a little bit better.

"We should continue our tour," she said.

Lara made a face. "Honestly, the stuff around here is hardly tour-worthy. What exactly do you want to see—the fine linoleum tables in the cafeteria? Or maybe the sweat-scented gym?"

"The cafeteria," Caroline replied, ignoring Lara's sarcasm. Perhaps the sights of Pinecone Arts Academy weren't exactly exciting, but she wanted to see the place where she'd be spending the next three years.

At that Lara took off at a brisk walk once more. Although Caroline tried to pay attention to the directions, she soon lost track amid the hallway maze. She could only hope that she'd be able to find places again without her sister as a guide. After all, middle school was her big chance to do things all by herself. Caroline did not intend to squander that opportunity.

"Here it is," Lara announced when they reached a set of double doors. "The cafeteria, in all its glory."

Caroline peeked in through the small window. Looking at the empty rows of chairs and tables, she tried to imagine the room full of chattering middle schoolers. Where would she sit? Probably not with Lara, since sixth graders and seventh graders had different lunch periods. Yet she couldn't imagine who else might sit with her, and her stomach turned.

"The food actually isn't terrible," Lara said. "Though I recommend avoiding the meatloaf at all costs. Your bowels will appreciate it."

Just as Caroline began to type a thanks for the bowel-saving advice, a clomping sound startled her. She swiveled her head to see a trio of kids—two boys and a girl—rounding the corner toward the cafeteria.

Caroline oftentimes felt as though an artist silently lurked in the back of her mind. Her artist painted and doodled and shaded with a perfect precision that she herself lacked. She didn't know if it was an autism thing or just an artist thing, but either way the artist had a way of knowing her feelings before she did. And right now, the artist was painting big, bold streaks of yellow and green.

This was Caroline's big chance to meet real Pinecone students. Kids who weren't related to her, kids who maybe could be her friends. She inhaled a deep breath and tapped a few buttons on her tablet. "Hello!"

The kids stared, and Caroline felt her heartbeat skitter. Of course they'd stare. They probably had never met someone like her before. Still, Caroline held out hope that they could get used to it. She stared at the tablet screen and tried to come up with the right words, words that might let them see that she was friend-worthy.

"Are you really talking to us?" the boy asked.

"Yes, she is. And when someone says hello to you, it's generally considered polite to say hi back," Lara said in her bossiest voice.

Caroline immediately shot her sister a Look. As much as the question hurt, she hardly thought that Lara's response would help improve the situation in any way. There was a lot Caroline didn't know about middle school, but she knew she didn't want her sister acting like a bossy busybody.

The boy glared at Lara—an understandable response, in Caroline's opinion. "Hey, look," he said. "I didn't mean anything by it."

"Yeah," one of the girls added. "We just wanted to know! I've never met anyone who . . . you know . . . talks that way."

"Well, now you have," Lara said. "And Caroline would certainly appreciate it if you didn't gawk at her like some kind of zoo exhibit."

Bouncing on her tiptoes, Caroline flapped her hands at a rapid speed. Why, oh why, did Lara have to be so very protective? Sure, the kids' ignorance was annoying, but Lara was even worse. Caroline could speak for herself! She didn't need her big sister to swoop in and save her from anything.

With so many bad emotions flooding her, Caroline could barely keep up with everything that was going on around her. The girl was saying something, but it was difficult for Caroline to pick up on every word.

"Whatever ... no offense ... freak out ..."

"I am not freaking out!" Lara said in a volume that suggested that she was on the verge of doing just that. "I just want you to apologize to my sister."

Caroline put considerable effort toward not screaming as she mashed buttons on her tablet. The artist in the back of her brain started sketching messy scrawls in black and gray.

"No no no no no," Caroline said. At times like these, the "no" button in her app was quite useful. All of this was moving way too fast for her to type out a proper response. Hopefully "no" would get the message across.

Caroline cradled her head in her hands and tugged at her hair. She wanted the sensation of ripped hair, painful though it was. But she had just enough awareness to know that actually doing so would be a very, very bad idea. To calm herself, she tried humming her favorite pop song.

"I think you've done quite enough," Lara told the group, her voice cold. "Maybe you should get out of here."

They did. As the kids scampered away, all Caroline could think was that they most definitely were not going to be her friends now. And it was all thanks to Lara and her big mouth.

CHAPTER THREE:

THE CASE OF THE IRRITABLE LITTLE SISTER

For as long as she could remember, Lara had looked after Caroline. No one asked her to do it. It just felt right to her. Even before Caroline learned how to talk with her tablet, Lara could sometimes guess what her sister wanted to say. Her accuracy rate wasn't perfect, but she was better at it than anyone else. Even Dad and Ima.

These days Caroline didn't need Lara to be her translator. That was good, of course. Still. When awful kids were being awful, why shouldn't Lara step in? It was her job as the older sister. Yet now Caroline was acting as though Lara had stepped on Kugel's tail. On purpose!

Caroline did not say a single word on the walk back to Principal Jenkins's office. Nor did she show any sign of talking once the car engine started humming and they began the ride home.

"I was just looking out for you," Lara repeated for approximately the seventy millionth time. "Those kids were being awfully rude."

Still nothing. Lara glanced over at her sister's tablet and saw that Caroline was deeply involved in a game of Candy Crush. She made no move to open her speech app. Okay. Fine. Maybe Caroline was mad now. But she couldn't possibly ignore Lara forever.

Yet as the evening wore on, it became apparent that Caroline's irritation had not gone away. Even Kugel, who usually favored Caroline, stayed clear of her.

Lara found her sister outside on the swing set, although she was not swinging so much as she was kicking her feet into the dirt.

"Hi," Lara said, staring at her sneakers.

Since this was a rare occasion when Caroline didn't have her tablet, she couldn't say anything back. That meant Lara could talk all she liked without worrying about being interrupted. Normally she didn't like to take advantage of this. But right now she had quite a lot to say.

"Look. I'm sorry. Well, I'm not sorry that I told those jerks off, because they deserved it. I'm sorry that you're hurt. Anyway, if you want to talk, you know where I am."

Lara trudged back to the house, fully expecting Caroline to stay put. To her surprise, footsteps followed only a few strides behind her. She turned to see Caroline flash a hand signal—the one that meant "wait."

As she waited for Caroline to retrieve her tablet, she considered how best to approach the situation. Clearly, she'd messed up. But if Caroline would just understand that she was only trying to help, then maybe . . .

"I don't need you."

Lara flinched at the words, even though Caroline's tablet-voice spoke without judgment. How could Caroline not need her? She was the older sister!

"I didn't ask for your help," Caroline continued.

"I had to!" Lara protested. "You're my sister and the way those kids were talking about you just wasn't right."

Lara could have said more. She wanted to say more. But Caroline was tapping furiously, and Lara doubted whether she could have said anything to make her slow down.

"You always try to fix things. But you can't fix everything, Lara."

Unbelievable! Lara just didn't get it. One minute Caroline was asking to share her tree—her personal tree!—and then the next she got all annoyed when Lara tried to do something nice for her. Sometimes Lara felt like she didn't understand her sister at all.

"I don't understand why you're so mad at me for trying to help." Lara tried to keep her voice even, like Caroline's computer voice. "I just thought that maybe if I told them that they were being rude, they would, you know, talk to you like a normal person."

"I am not a normal person," Caroline said. She continued to tap away furiously at her screen. "And I know how to deal with people being rude."

"Yes, but you shouldn't have to! I just wanted to help."

Caroline drew her face into a pout and did not touch her tablet for eons, although Lara supposed the silence probably only lasted for mere seconds. Finally, she started typing again.

"You don't know anything, Lara Finkel. You can't help anyone. You definitely can't help me."

Lara opened her mouth. Tried to think of a smart comeback. Failed. And so she closed her mouth. Meanwhile, Caroline pranced away somewhere. She was probably off to bake challah with Aviva or something. Lara scowled at the very thought.

Never mind Caroline.

She, Lara, had plenty to do on her own.

Unfortunately, she failed to think of a single thing at the moment.

So she did what she always did when her feelings started to be too much. She went to her bookshelf and pulled out one of her Georgia Ketteridge books—number three, the best one in the series.

She tried to concentrate on the plot—a terribly exciting mystery that involved a series of kidnappings. But she couldn't. Thoughts of Caroline and school and everything that had been said kept invading her mind.

How would Georgia handle a moody little sister? It was hard to say. Georgia was an only child. Lucky her.

Ugh. There was no way Lara could concentrate on Georgia's adventures.

Glancing around the room, Lara's eyes landed upon her brand-new FIASCCO notebook. She'd only intended to use it for real mysteries, but of course she didn't have a real mystery yet. Besides, this was a mystery of sorts, wasn't it?

Before she could talk herself out of it, Lara grabbed her favorite purple pen and started scribbling in the notebook. Maybe Caroline wasn't a mystery exactly, but she might as well get in the practice of making detective-ish observations.

Lara began to write.

LOCATION: Pinecone Arts Academy, approximately 3:00 p.m.

EVENT: I, Lara Finkel, attempted to rescue C. from potential criminals (*rude middle school students, which is practically the same thing*). C. very irritable in response.

ADDITIONAL OBSERVATION: C. also mad that she wasn't included in establishment of FIASCCO. This suggests that she does, in fact, want to do things with me. Except she also said she doesn't need me.

CONCLUSION: C. makes no sense.

QUESTION FOR FURTHER INVESTIGATION: Why doesn't my sister realize that I am trying to help her?

CHAPTER FOUR:

SHABBAT RUCKUS

Caroline waited for Lara to apologize, but no such thing occurred. The day after their fight, Lara admitted that she "could have handled the whole situation a little better, maybe."

It was something. But she still didn't say the words Caroline really wanted to hear: "I'm sorry." She certainly didn't say "I'll try not to do that again." Apparently, such words were not in Lara's otherwise large vocabulary.

Whenever Caroline thought about it, she just got mad all over again. So she tried not to think about it. She had far too much to worry about as it was. In less than a week, she'd be going to middle school for real. For now, she preferred not to continue fighting with Lara. She wanted to enjoy these last few days of summer.

Tonight's order of business: Shabbat dinner with the whole family.

The state of the kitchen could be fairly described as a ruckus. Caroline usually preferred to avoid ruckus. But ruckus with family and good food was another matter, and so she always looked forward to Shabbat dinners.

In one corner of the kitchen, her little brother played with his toy trucks. Despite the fact that Dad and Ima didn't allow toys in the kitchen, Benny vroom-vroomed in what most certainly was not an inside voice. Benny didn't have an inside voice.

Dad was busy at the stove, muttering to himself as he stirred at the pot. That was pretty Dad-like, though Caroline noticed his curly hair was sticking up and his shirt was all wrinkly. Ima wouldn't like that.

Caroline herself sat on top of the kitchen table. This too was against family rules, but Dad never enforced them as rigorously as Ima did. Her tablet sat to the side as she cradled her sketchpad.

Chewing on the end of her pencil, Caroline considered her drawing. She'd had every intention of sketching a rhinoceros, but so far it resembled a weirdly shaped cloud. She could do better, if only—

"What are you drawing, Lina-Lin?" Lara asked.

Caroline looked up and smiled at her sister. Maybe this time Lara would really, truly apologize. And then things could be good again, couldn't they?

"Just a practice drawing, and obviously not a good one," Caroline replied. Unable to bear the sight of the malformed rhinoceros any longer, Caroline shut her sketch-book. "How is the detective agency?" she asked Lara.

When she first discovered that Lara had plastered the whole neighborhood in FIASCCO flyers, Caroline had felt a slight—okay, maybe not so slight—pang. That was just the sort of thing they used to do together, as Lara-and-Caroline. She didn't understand why Lara wanted to be just Lara, on her own. Caroline decided she would get involved with FIASCCO business anyway. As soon as FIASCCO got its first case, Caroline would be there to offer her assistance to a grateful Lara. That was the plan.

If FIASCCO got its first case. Caroline didn't often doubt Lara, who had a way of making impossible things seem not only possible, but likely. Yet when it came to FIASCCO, Caroline wasn't so sure.

"That's not really any of your business," Lara said shortly. "But it's fine. Going great."

Well, that confirmed the doubts. Normally Lara loved the opportunity to talk about anything related to Georgia Ketteridge and detecting in general.

"I have ideas for mysteries for you to solve," Caroline said. "I made a list. Do you want to see?"

"No! I mean, it's nice of you to try. But I want to find a mystery on my own. It probably took Georgia Ketteridge a while to get her first mystery, too. I'll find one soon."

Caroline just sighed and tapped the "okay" button. There wasn't much use arguing with Lara when she got into one of her moods.

A loud voice sounded from the direction of the stove—and the words definitely were not Ima-approved.

"Dad used a bad word!" Benny chanted. "What's your punishment gonna be?"

Wincing, Dad wiped a layer of sweat off his forehead. "I know, I know. That was bad, very bad. It's just . . . NOT THE STRING BEANS!"

Everybody stared at Dad, and Caroline felt her pulse quicken.

"I'm fine, I'm fine!" Dad said quickly. "Don't worry about me. Every culinary masterpiece requires some sweat and tears."

Caroline wasn't so sure, but she turned her attention away from Dad and toward her sister. Lara still looked decidedly grumpy. Caroline studied her sister's pouty lips, the slight crinkle to her nose.

Even before the current FIASCCO fiasco, Caroline had sensed that Lara was in a never-ending bad mood. The cause of said mood remained a mystery, but it was hard to ignore the facts.

Fact #1: Lara had developed a habit of glaring at people for seemingly no reason whatsoever. By Caroline's count, she glared three times per hour. At least.

Fact #2: For the past several months, Lara had stopped reading excerpts of the Georgia Ketteridge books to Caroline before bed. They'd left off at an exciting scene where Georgia was interrogating the top suspect, but Lara didn't care. Caroline had eventually borrowed the book and finished it for herself.

And, of course, there was Fact #3: Lara didn't seem particularly excited about Shabbat, even though a big white cheesecake box was in the back of the refrigerator. This was in spite of the fact that Lara loved cheesecake more than any other Finkel.

Clearly, something was wrong with Lara. Caroline suspected that the beginning of Lara's grumpiness coincided with the arrival of their cousin Aviva from Israel. It didn't make much sense. She herself was quite fond of Aviva. Lara would be too, if she'd just give Aviva a chance and stop being weird.

As if to prove Caroline's suspicion, Aviva strolled into the kitchen and Lara's lips gave an unhappy twitch. "Hello, cousins!" Aviva said, smiling brightly.

Since Aviva was from Israel, she spoke with an accent.

Caroline thought it sounded cool. She'd even tried to see if she could switch her voice app to an Israeli accent instead of a British one, but the app had a rather limited number of voices to choose from. She'd been using the tablet since she was five, but a few months ago Caroline had switched to the British-lady voice because it made her sound grown-up. When you were an eleven-year-old girl who talked with a tablet, sounding grown-up was a very good thing.

"Hi," Caroline said.

She nudged Lara, who mumbled a greeting. Caroline barely repressed a sigh. Really, her sister's treatment of Aviva embarrassed her. She knew it embarrassed Ima, too.

"How is your detective agency going?" Aviva asked. "Fiasco?"

"Actually, it's *F-I-A-S-C-C-O*," Lara corrected. "And it's going great, thank you!"

"That's nice. Do you have a case?"

"Not that it's any of your business, but yes. I can't talk about it to you, though. Top secret information!"

Caroline stared at her sister. She felt reasonably certain that Lara had just made the whole thing up. Otherwise known as lying.

Lara was many things, but Caroline had never thought

36

of her sister as a liar. Frowning, Caroline opened her sketchbook. Wrestling with the not-rhinoceros was more appealing than trying to make sense of her sister and Aviva's relationship.

She glanced out the window. Sunset wouldn't be for another few hours yet, but they'd probably start Shabbat dinner soon anyway. Technically, people weren't supposed to start Shabbat until sunset on Friday night. But Ima said that Seattle summers had so much daylight that dinner couldn't possibly wait for the sun to finish its business. Caroline's growling stomach quite agreed.

As Ima and Noah and Aunt Miriam joined everyone else in the kitchen, Caroline relaxed her shoulders. Yes, Lara was acting weird, and yes, she and Aviva had some kind of ridiculous feud going on. But for now, Caroline just wanted to enjoy Shabbat with her family.

She'd watch out for a good mystery during dinner.

CHAPTER FIVE:

IN WHICH A MYSTERY PRESENTS ITSELF

LOCATION: Kitchen (5:00 p.m., Shabbat)

EVENT: Dad got angry about something that involves string beans. Very Bad Words were involved.

QUESTION FOR FURTHER INVESTIGATION: Probably nothing. I really wish there was a better mystery around here. It's been days since I put up my flyers and absolutely nothing has happened yet. Blech!

The Finkels chanted the Hamotzi their way. Which is to say that Benny was a half-beat faster than everyone else, while Caroline's British-lady computer voice strayed several measures behind. Just about everyone sang in a different key, making it impossible to say who was or was not in tune. (Lara thought Aviva sounded even more out of tune than the rest of them. Very nicely, she kept the thought to herself.)

Once they completed the blessings, pandemonium broke out as everyone rushed for the food. Lara placed a generously sized helping of brisket on her plate. On the other side of the table, Aviva frowned at the food.

Lara glared at her cousin. It would be just like Aviva to say something nasty about Dad's undoubtedly delicious food.

In the Finkel household, it was an established fact that whenever Dad made Shabbat dinner, it would taste good.

"More Ashkenazi food, I know," Dad said. "I'm still working on perfecting my Sephardic cuisine so I can make it for you guys. In the meantime, no one wants to eat deconstructed spanakopita."

He looked at Aviva and Aunt Miriam as he spoke. Ever since arriving from Israel six months ago, Aviva hadn't exactly been subtle in expressing her opinions about American food. Or anything else, for that matter. According to Aviva, the falafel was warmer in Israel. The street music, livelier. The pillows, fluffier. (Well, okay, so Aviva hadn't actually said that last one. Yet. It was probably only a matter of time.) Personally, Lara thought Aviva should just go back to Israel if everything was so much better there.

"The food is excellent, I'm sure," Aunt Miriam said in her melodic accent. "We are becoming used to America, and that means Ashkenazi food."

Aviva coughed from her end of the table, and Lara glared at her once more.

Lara knew that brisket was an Ashkenazi food. So was matzo ball soup and noodle kugel and all of the other Jewish foods Dad made for them using Grandma Lynne's cookbook. Since Ima and Aunt Miriam were Sephardic Jews, they had recipes for grape leaves, walnut spice cake, and other delicious things. The difference was that Dad's grandparents came from Russia, while Ima had immigrated to Israel from Turkey as a child. Ima told Lara that they were descended from Jews who were expelled from Spain and Portugal in 1492. Dad's family came from a different group of Jews. "We are different branches from the same tree," she had explained.

That meant that the Finkel children—Lara and Caroline and their brothers—were like the base of the tree, where the Ashkenazi branch and the Sephardic branch came together. Lara always thought that was pretty cool. Noah called them "Ashkephardic."

Regardless, Lara could not understand why Aviva had to be such a snob about brisket. So maybe moving to a new country at the age of twelve wasn't easy. Fine. But that didn't give Aviva the right to be so very annoying.

"I'm sure your food is absolutely delicious, Dad. It always is." Lara made sure to look in Aviva's general direction as she spoke.

Yet when Lara put the first forkful of brisket into her mouth, it took all of her willpower to avoid spitting it right back out.

Biting into the meat felt like chewing on a dirty sock—not that Lara had ever done such a thing, of course. But she imagined that a sock might also flap around unpleasantly in her mouth, infecting her taste buds with its foulness.

The brisket tasted too salty, yet it also lacked flavor. The meat felt too dry, the sauce too watery. The edges of the brisket were completely hard, while the center looked practically raw. The whole thing was, quite simply, disgusting. Horrible. Gross.

A quick look around the table revealed that everyone else knew it too. Noah downed a glassful of water. Caroline pushed her plate several inches away. Aviva twisted her face up into an unmistakable grimace.

As usual, Benny said what everyone else was thinking. "Dad, this stuff tastes like something Kugel spit up. Guh-ross."

Dad didn't deny it. "I'm so sorry, everyone. I have no idea what happened. Probably just a bad ADHD day for me." His eyes darted around the table, a weak smile struggling to stay on his face. "Lucky that we have so much other food here!"

Only they didn't. Not really. The noodle kugel turned out to be overcooked, while the string beans reeked of lemons. That left them with a whole lot of salad and not much else. Lara held the very sensible opinion that only having salad for dinner was a full-fledged tragedy.

"I'm sorry, guys," Dad said, over and over again.

"It is all right, Joseph," Ima said. But her accent thickened, as it always did whenever she was worried. Lara frowned. None of this felt quite right. "How about we order pizza?"

"On Shabbat?" Aviva said.

Lara's irritation with her cousin flared up again. Okay, yes. Pizza wasn't exactly traditional. But so what?

"Pizza is absolutely delicious," Lara pronounced.

A slight frown lingered on Aviva's face, but she didn't say anything else. Good.

In truth, Lara thought pizza on Shabbat felt a little weird too, but she wasn't going to say so. Not when Dad still looked so out of it.

Ima squeezed Dad's shoulder. "Pizza Shabbat will be a new experience, yes?"

"You know how I love doing new and weird things," he replied. He smiled slightly, staring at Ima with one of those lovey-dovey looks that bordered on gross.

And so it was decided that this would be the first-ever pizza Shabbat. After some heated debate, Ima placed an order for three large pies with vegetarian toppings, therefore making their pizza a kosher meal. Even Aviva no longer seemed bothered with the change in the menu.

By the time the pizza arrived, everyone was chattering happily. As Lara took a big bite of her first slice, Caroline bounced over. Her own cheeks were puffed out with food. Caroline tapped away on her tablet while she chewed. One of the advantages of Caroline's communication method was her ability to talk and eat at the same time without subjecting anyone to the sight of half-chewed food.

Caroline's face hardly moved at all while she typed. "You want a mystery to solve."

"Yes," Lara said through a mouthful of cheese. "Why?"

"I have one for you. A very important mystery."

Her little sister had some big mystery? Hmm. Lara couldn't imagine it would be any good, on account of

Caroline being eleven and not an expert detective at all. She was pretty sure Caroline hadn't even read all the Georgia books!

Still, it wasn't as though FIASCCO had a ton of cases to choose from at the moment. Lara had exaggerated when she'd told Aviva she was already working on a case. Just a bit! Aviva being Aviva, she'd probably ask about it soon and then Lara would have to lie again. Not great.

Lara considered. She needed all the leads she could get.

"Okay. What's the big mystery?" she asked.

Caroline's mouth was pressed into a thin line as her fingers flew across the screen.

"You need to find out why Dad made yucky brisket tonight."

CHAPTER SIX:

YOUNGER SISTER PROBLEMS

Caroline saw things. Some people failed to recognize this rather basic fact, mistaking her lack of mouth-words for a lack of thoughts. Caroline actually had loads of thoughts, thank you very much. Sometimes she typed them out on her tablet, sometimes she kept them to herself. But she always saw things.

That's how she knew that Dad's mistake with the brisket might be worthy of investigation.

Lara, however, looked doubtful. "I don't think bad brisket is exactly mysterious. He said he was having a bad ADHD day. Case closed. Besides, would Georgia Ketteridge spend an entire book investigating brisket?"

"She's not Jewish," Caroline pointed out. She was pretty sure that brisket was a Jewish thing.

"I don't think Georgia would investigate bad ham, either," Lara insisted.

Caroline sighed. No matter what Lara thought, she'd known the moment she'd bitten into the gross brisket that it meant something. She just didn't know what.

Why wouldn't her sister listen to her? Just because she was a year younger and couldn't take charge of things in a Lara-like way didn't mean she couldn't do anything. As much as Caroline loved her sister—and she did!—sometimes she couldn't help but feel like Lara thought she lived in a Georgia Ketteridge novel. Lara, of course, was Georgia. Caroline? She was lucky to be a sidekick.

Lara folded her arms across her chest, head high. "I didn't want to investigate family things," she said. "I already know everything about us. What's there to investigate?"

Caroline doubted that Lara knew nearly as much about the Finkels as she claimed, but decided not to pursue the argument.

"Think about it," she said. "Sure, Dad has ADHD. But when has Dad ever made bad food?"

"Last Purim. Those hamantaschen were like clay bricks."

"That doesn't count! Benny mixed plaster powder into the flour as a joke."

The memory made Caroline giggle. Lara, however, clearly was not in the mood for amusement.

Caroline inhaled deeply before starting to type again.

"It's not just the brisket," she told Lara. "Dad's done a bunch of weird things lately."

"Really? I haven't noticed."

Not typing out a snarky remark required Caroline to exercise considerable restraint. Of course Lara hadn't noticed anything amiss with Dad. She had been far too busy moping over the failure of FIASCCO and Aviva's existence and who knows what else.

So Caroline took it upon herself to recite the long list of evidence that there was, in fact, something weird with Dad.

#1: He'd been nearly forty minutes late picking them up at day camp last Tuesday.

#2: On Thursday night, he hadn't been at all interested in watching *Family Cooking Extravaganza* with everyone else. Normally, Dad made special popcorn just for the occasion. This week? Nothing.

And, of course, there was #3: The door to Dad's office had remained completely shut every day for two full weeks—even on the weekends! Normal Dad left the door open most of the time so that the kids (and Kugel) could wander in and say hello. Weird Dad kept himself locked in there for hours, only emerging when Ima asked him to.

Lara made a face, and Caroline knew that even this evidence hadn't been enough to convince her sister.

"Come on," Caroline prodded. "It will be fun. And it's not like you have anything else to investigate right now."

That prompted another face from Lara, this one decidedly more unpleasant. But after a moment, she nodded. "Okay. You're right. I didn't really plan to investigate minor family matters, but since you're the only one to ask for help from FIASCCO, I'll do it. I will solve the case of the gross brisket."

"You mean we'll solve it," Caroline corrected. "It's called the Finkel Investigation Agency Solving Consequential Crimes Only, right?"

"Yes, so?"

"So, I'm a Finkel."

"Sooo?" Lara said. "FIASCCO is my agency."

"And investigating Dad was my idea."

For a long moment, neither of them said anything. They just sat in tense silence while Caroline stared at her speech app, trying to come up with magic words that would somehow make her sister understand why she wanted—no, needed—to be part of FIASCCO too.

Finally, Lara nodded. "Okay. Fine. You are officially part of this investigation as a junior detective."

She was less than thrilled about the *junior* part, but Caroline would take it.

It turned out that investigating Dad was difficult business.

The first and biggest problem was that Dad basically lived in his office these days. Caroline and Lara could hardly sneak behind his back when his back was, well, right there!

Luckily, an opportunity arrived early in the morning on Day 5 of the investigation. Like many other unexpected events in the Finkel household, it was all thanks to Benny.

Caroline had only been awake for fifteen minutes when a loud crash sounded from the backyard. It was quickly followed by a high-pitched yelp.

She hurried to the patio in her nightshirt. Everyone else was there in similar states of just-got-out-of-bed-ness. Aunt Miriam looked particularly ridiculous in fluffy purple slippers.

And then there was Benny, sprawled out on the grass completely unmoving. There was something unsettling, Caroline thought, about a still Benny.

Ima rushed forward, and within an instant she became Dr. Ima, talking rapidly about bones and fractures and other medical-y things that made Caroline's stomach turn.

Benny's eyes flew open. "I fell out of the tree," he announced, rather unnecessarily.

"Obviously," Ima said, the lines around her mouth disappearing into her skin. "Though I think the more relevant issue is what you were doing up there in the first place."

Caroline didn't quite make out Benny's rambling answer, but it seemed to involve some kind of treehouse-building effort. She released a breath and turned toward Lara, whose face was several shades paler than usual. Lara often got weird when someone was hurt, even though Benny wasn't even bleeding.

Sometimes Caroline wondered why her squeamish sister wanted to investigate grossness as a career, though she didn't dare say it out loud.

After Ima fussed for several minutes, it was decided that she and Dad would accompany Benny to the emergency room right away. He protested, but Ima would not be swayed on the matter.

"He'll be okay," Caroline said to her sister. "Ima's just being a doctor again."

"Yeah," Lara said. But her voice shook ever so slightly.

Lara still seemed a little out of sorts when the station

wagon chugged out of the driveway, but she looked at Caroline and managed a weak grin. "This is our chance to investigate. Dad's office, stat."

Even though she didn't really understand what *stat* meant, Caroline smiled. This was exactly what she'd been waiting for: a chance to prove herself indispensable to Lara.

As the sisters headed straight for Dad's office, Caroline held her breath. Barging right through the door when Dad wasn't there felt a little scandalous—this was something the Finkel children Did Not Do.

"Stage one complete. Now you can take watch by the door," Lara said.

The order was ridiculous. Giving Lara her very best glare, Caroline grabbed her tablet and started tapping at top speed.

"We don't need a lookout. Dad and Ima are gone."

"Lookout is a very important job," Lara protested. "Besides, you can never be too careful. Georgia usually has a lookout."

Caroline glared again.

"Okay, okay," Lara said. "We'll do this together. But we need to stay alert for intruders."

They began to paw through the skyscraper-sized mound

of papers on Dad's desk. Dad, apparently, never saw the need to throw things away. Nor did he bother to arrange his things in anything that remotely resembled order. Loose sheets of paper stuck out every which way from towering stacks, which teetered on the verge of total collapse.

Lara sighed at the sight. "Oh, Dad," she said.

Most of Dad's papers were boring—bills and invoices and other adult-ish things. But one piece of paper grabbed Caroline's attention. It looked just like a dozen other papers in the stack, save for the words stamped in bold type across the top. It just looked sinister somehow, even though Caroline wasn't quite sure what it all meant. She gulped.

"What does *severance* mean?" she asked Lara.

"I'm not entirely sure," Lara said. "I know that *sever* means to cut something off. Like a severed head. But why are you asking about severing things? This isn't supposed to be that kind of mystery!"

Lara shuddered dramatically. Caroline just frowned. She was pretty sure this piece of paper didn't have anything to do with wayward body parts. But what *did* it mean?

"We don't know what kind of mystery this is," Caroline said.

She shoved the piece of paper toward Lara. As her sister read, trouble crept into her face, wrinkling her forehead. Lara's eyebrows danced up, up, and up.

Caroline did not like that look one bit. The canvas in her mind flashed red, then pitch-black.

Finally, Lara spoke again. "Lina, this is bad. Really, really bad."

Caroline typed a single word on her tablet: "What?"

"I think . . . I think Dad lost his job."

Oh.

Oh no.

CHAPTER SEVEN:

CRACKING THE CASE

LOCATION: Dad's office, noon.

EVENT: C. and I found a piece of paper in Dad's office. It says SEVERANCE PAYMENT.

CONCLUSION: Dad got fired and didn't tell us about it.

QUESTION FOR FURTHER INVESTIGATION: Why can't Dad tell us the truth?

Lara's mind burst with thoughts, but one kept circling back to her. This was not how her very first investigation was supposed to go.

In Georgia Ketteridge books, solving mysteries was always fun. Sure, Georgia might get trapped in a cellar for a few hours on occasion. And there was that one time when she broke her arm after a rather suspicious fall in a dark cave.

Yet Georgia never got an awful, twisting feeling in her gut. The feeling that maybe she shouldn't have started investigating something at all.

The feeling that Lara now couldn't shake off.

She hadn't wanted to believe it. But the paper Caroline found was perfectly clear. Two weeks ago, Dad had been "terminated." (What a horrible word! But Lara supposed that horrible things needed horrible words.)

As she read further, she filed away more information in her mind. Dad's newspaper had fired him two weeks ago. They'd given him something called a severance package, which seemed to mean he got a lot of money. It was a staggering number that had to be more allowance than Lara would ever get in her whole life. But still. Fired meant fired.

That was why Dad burned the brisket. He must have been ... distracted.

Lara flapped her fingers. Dad's job at the newspaper was supposed to be the one that worked out for him. He'd had it for nearly three whole years. Whenever he talked about work, he went on about how much he liked his boss and his stories. "The best job in the world," he'd say, "apart from being a dad, of course," and the whole thing was so cheesy that Lara groaned on principle.

Dad getting fired from the best job in the world was not supposed to happen. But it did, and now it couldn't un-happen.

"Why didn't Dad tell us?" Lara wondered out loud. "Not telling something important is basically the same as lying."

Caroline did not respond for a long while. It was so long that Lara thought maybe she'd gone into a not-talking mood. But eventually Caroline spoke. "I don't like it either. But maybe there's a reason Dad didn't tell us about it."

"And what would that be?" Lara asked, still cross.

This time, Caroline's response came much more quickly. "Maybe it has something to do with the reason why he got fired."

Lara locked her gaze on her sister. Caroline was right. The reason behind Dad's firing probably was important. Did he make a mistake in one of his stories? No, Dad would never. Maybe he'd written something that a powerful person didn't like. Dad was always complaining about "the higher-ups" at his newspaper and how they wanted to control things. Yes. That had to be it.

Still, Lara wished she knew for sure. She did not care at all for the not-knowing feeling. Wanting to know things was precisely why she'd become a detective in the first place. She hadn't realized that answering one question would lead to so many more. Was this what real detectives did? Enter an endless spiral of questions, one after another?

"Ima probably knows," Caroline continued. "Maybe they just don't want us to worry."

It made sense. And yet Lara couldn't shake the Very Bad Feeling from her gut.

"Don't you remember what happened last time Dad lost his job?" Lara asked.

"Not really."

Lara stared at her sister. As a nine-year-old, Lara had only been a little kid when it happened, but she doubted that the memories would ever go away.

At first she'd thought the whole thing would be fun. If Dad was going to stay at home during the day instead of going to work, that meant he would have more time to play with her. Cook her favorite foods. Listen to her detailed accounts of life in fourth grade.

Only it didn't happen. In fact, Dad didn't play with her at all during those long months. He didn't cook much, either, leaving everyone to suffer through microwaved dinners and Ima's questionable attempts at cooking. And whenever Lara tried to talk to him about her days, he never asked questions or laughed at the proper places in her stories. He just sat there on the couch, fiddling with his hands and staring at the TV screen.

Then Dad got his job at the newspaper and things got

better again. It didn't happen all at once, but soon enough life in the Finkel family was normal. Or about as normal as it ever got. And Lara could almost—but not quite—forget that her dad had ever spent days at a time in his pajamas, watching game shows on TV.

There had been only one bright spot to the whole experience: Georgia Ketteridge. Lara read her first Georgia book a month after Dad lost his job. Within four days, she'd finished the entire series and started her first of many rereads. Maybe she didn't have her father, but at least she'd had Georgia. In Georgia's world, dads didn't start acting scarily weird all of a sudden. Her dad certainly would not lose his job, ever. And even when things got really, really bad for Georgia, everything worked itself out by the end of the book. Always.

Yet apparently none of these events had made much of an impression on Caroline.

"You really don't remember it at all?" Lara asked her sister. "Dad was . . . weird. Ima too. That was the only time Ima ever let us have mac and cheese out of the box for dinner. Which we had about three times a week."

Caroline frowned. "I remember the mac and cheese. I never liked the box stuff."

"Well, you'll probably need to get used to it," Lara said,

thinking back to the ruined brisket. "At least until Dad gets a new job. Or Ima learns how to use the oven. Which will probably happen at around the same time Kugel gives up shrimp and goes kosher."

"Oh," Caroline said.

That was all—*oh*. Well, Lara understood her sister's feelings. "We need to do something," she declared.

Caroline tapped her tablet for quite a while, but decided against actually saying anything. Lara often envied her sister's way of communicating. She could think of more than a few occasions when deleting her words would have been quite useful. But sometimes not knowing what Caroline wanted to say was just plain annoying.

"Are you sure?"

"Yes! We may have completed the first phase of the investigation, but FIASCCO's work isn't done. Not while there are still loose ends."

Georgia always talked about the need to tie up loose ends. Lara figured that there were plenty of those in the Case of the Gross Brisket.

"But we already solved the mystery. Right?" Caroline asked.

She had a point. But Lara wasn't about to admit it. If

she were being perfectly honestly, it stung a little that Caroline had figured out that something might be wrong with Dad before she herself had noticed. Caroline didn't even want to be a detective! Not like Lara did. Now it was *her* turn to decide on a mission for *her* detective agency.

"We don't know why Dad lost his job," Lara pointed out. "That's part of the case."

"I guess so. But I'm not sure how we can find out more than we already know, and besides, aren't we going to be busy? You know, with school."

Lara scoffed. "We won't be in school all day. There's no reason for it to intrude on FIASCCO business. But if you don't want to be involved anymore, you can just say so."

"That's not what I meant!"

"Well, it sure sounded like it," Lara told her.

A fierce frown still glued to her face, Caroline paused in the middle of typing her response. "Do you hear something?"

Lara tried to silence her thoughts and listen to the outside world. Sure enough, footsteps echoed from downstairs, accompanied by loud Benny-chatter.

"We need to get out of here ASAP," Lara said.

Caroline nodded and slid toward the door. Lara took one last look around the disorganized office and sighed.

By all rights, their progress in the investigation should be a cause for celebration. Yet Lara felt as though boulders were tied to her feet as she scurried away from her father's office.

CHAPTER EIGHT:

WORDS AND WORRIES

Caroline thought perhaps that discovering the truth about Dad would change everything right away. But for the next week, life in the Finkel household plodded on more or less as usual. Benny still raced around with his toy cars. Noah still spent most evenings away with his friends, returning just before the curfew Ima set. Lara and Aviva still bickered over issues both large and small. (Their most recent kerfuffle erupted when Aviva tried to instruct the rest of the family on the correct way to prepare hummus.)

Soon, a very big distraction from the Dad problem began to eat up more and more of Caroline's thoughts.

Tomorrow, Caroline would officially be a middle school student. Tomorrow, everything would change. And so tonight was one of those nights when sleep was quite impossible. There were far too many thoughts flitting around Caroline's mind, each one spawning another chain of thoughts until she just about burst with worries— dark splatters of paint blotting a perfect white canvas.

Within the splotches of brown and black, she saw a classroom of kids laughing at her. She saw herself sitting alone at lunch, everyone whispering and pointing. She saw Principal Jenkins, looking at her with pitying eyes as she explained that she was very sorry, but girls like Caroline just weren't suitable for Pinecone Arts Academy.

Caroline rolled over. In the dark she could just barely make out the huddled mass of blankets on the other bed, swaying from side to side. She grabbed her tablet off the floor.

"Lara?" she asked. "Are you up?"

"Yes. What's going on, Lina-Lin?"

"What is middle school like?" Caroline asked. Most of her thoughts kept going back in that rather terrifying direction.

A huff came from the other bed. "It's middle school. There are classes and some of them are good. Some of them aren't. Watch out for gym. You should cross your fingers and hope you end up with Mr. Locke for that one. He's the nice one, even though he doesn't look like it."

Caroline had not previously given much thought to gym class at all, but the news that only one gym teacher could be described as nice alarmed her. Still, that wasn't really what she wanted to know.

She stared at her tablet screen and debated how best to approach her real question. Ultimately, she decided to just say it. "What about the other kids?"

Lara paused for a longer-than-normal amount of time before answering. "It's not really that different from elementary school. All right, well, maybe it is, but there are still good people and not-so-good people. You just have to find the good ones, Lina-Lin."

"And the not-good ones?"

"Those we avoid. By any means necessary."

Caroline thought about the matter. Things didn't sound quite so terrible when you put it that way. Although she couldn't help but wonder how, precisely, one might go about avoiding the not-good people. Lara's tour of Pinecone Arts Academy had not included any secret passageways that one could just slip into whenever a pesky person happened to be around.

Still, Lara was trying to be reassuring, and she appreciated that. "Okay," she said.

Silence descended upon the room, and it went on for so long that Caroline thought maybe her sister had managed to drift off into sleep after all.

Then Lara spoke again, voice quieter. "Look. I'm not going to tell you a bunch of lies just to make you feel better. Middle school is . . . well, middle school. It's not always fun and some of the kids are real jerks. I'd be happy to give you a list of the worst ones, though that would only cover the ones in my grade. Well, and a few of the eighth graders that are especially jerky."

Caroline snorted at the idea of a jerky-people list. It was such a Lara thing to do.

"But it's going to be okay," Lara continued. "I'll be there if you need anything, and most of the teachers are okay, really. If anyone gives you a hard time, just tell one of them. Or better yet, tell me. I'll make sure they don't try anything."

Caroline ran a hand through her hair. She appreciated Lara's need to protect her. Really, she did.

But she most certainly did not want to begin her life in middle school by running to a teacher for help—or worse still, her big sister. The memory of their visit to the school was enough to make Caroline antsy. That couldn't happen again.

Maybe Caroline would always be the girl who didn't talk with mouth-words, but she did not have to be the girl who went to other people to fix her own problems. She might not feel sure of very many things right now, but on this point she was quite certain.

Caroline wasn't in the mood to get into another argument, so she just pressed the "okay" button on her tablet.

The bundle of blankets that was Lara relaxed a bit. "Okay," Lara repeated. "It's going to be fine, Lina-Lin. Now we really should go to sleep. Or at least we should try."

Caroline tried. But it would be at least an hour before her mind became calm enough for true slumber.

* * *

LOCATION: *Dad's car, 7:30 a.m. (first day of school)*

EVENT: *C. and A. not here yet. Very annoying!*

QUESTION FOR FURTHER INVESTIGATION: *What should I do to help C. at school?*

"Excited for the first day of school, Lara-bear?" Dad asked as he gathered up the trash that had accumulated in the front seat of the car. Lara had been observing him closely for the past week. He looked quite normal-ish at the moment. Not at all like someone who had just lost a job he loved. Well, that was good at least.

Lara frowned as she considered the question. Maybe it was uncool of her, but she generally enjoyed school, with the notable exception of gym class. So the prospect of starting a whole new year ought to be exciting. But when she thought about it, the only thing she really felt was tiredness. And worry. Caroline had sounded awfully scared last night, and why shouldn't she be? Middle school was scary, even if you didn't talk with a computer voice.

But Dad didn't need to worry about her in addition to everything else, so Lara forced a smile. "Sure. I'm excited. Can't you see how excited I am?"

Her father frowned but didn't press the issue. "Fantastic. Now that your sister is going to be at the same school, you'll need to look out for her. I can count on you for that, right?"

Remembering their ill-fated visit to school, Lara couldn't help but think that Caroline would be less than thrilled about being looked out for. Then again, last night she welcomed Lara's sisterly advice. So who knew, really?

Lara nodded. "Sure. I'll make sure Caroline doesn't get into too much trouble."

Dad laughed at the undeniably ridiculous idea of Caroline getting into trouble.

While he was still chuckling, Aviva bounced up to the car and into the back seat. "Hi, Lara!" she said, with far more cheer than anyone should display before ten o'clock. "I can't wait for school. I think we're going to have some classes together. That's going to be so much fun!"

"Uh-huh," Lara mumbled. That was her maximum enthusiasm level for the moment.

A few minutes later Caroline joined them. Lara glanced backward at her sister and gave her what was hopefully a reassuring smile. Caroline did not return it.

Neither sister said much as Aviva began a one-sided conversation about what classes she was taking this year and how much she looked forward to taking eighth-grade advanced math. Show-off.

Still, the constant chatter lulled Lara into a normal mood. This was just school, after all.

They arrived at the academy and Dad let them out of the car with a (rather optimistic) proclamation that they would have a wonderful day. Yet even as the station wagon chugged away, Caroline hardly budged from her spot by the curb. She hugged her arms close to her chest—a sure sign of nerves.

Lara tried another smile. She pointed toward the squat brick building. "The school is that way. We can go in together."

Caroline didn't have her tablet out, so she couldn't communicate with words. But the grimace on her face spoke just as clearly as her app ever could: No way.

"Come on," Lara prodded. "Will you at least talk to me?"

Although Caroline gave a rather childish pout, she finally pulled her tablet out of her bag. "I'm fine, Lara. I don't need your help. You should do what you normally do when I'm not here."

"Fine," Lara said. She tried and failed not to feel hurt by the brush-off. "Have a nice day, then."

No response.

So much for looking out for her sister.

CHAPTER NINE:

HELENA THE ZEBRA

An hour into her first day, Caroline had tentatively reached the conclusion that middle school probably was not terrible. Although she hadn't yet identified a strong candidate for a friend, she had thoroughly enjoyed social studies class, which had included a fun map-drawing activity. Better still, she had her Experimental Art class now. Although she was not quite sure what the *experimental* part of Experimental Art meant, she figured that her future friend probably took art too.

All the excitement proved so distracting that Caroline got lost twice on her way to the classroom. An embarrassment, to be sure, but she was here now.

A pink-haired woman at the front of the room turned toward Caroline with a wide smile. "Hello! And who are you?"

Caroline considered the options. Without her tablet she couldn't really answer the question. She'd put the tablet away to give her neck a bit of a rest. So she just pointed to herself and hoped that Ms. Pink Hair would understand.

"Oh! You're Caroline Finkel, aren't you?" Somehow, the woman's smile became even wider. "Awesome! Why don't you find a seat now?"

The teacher pointed toward a blue table and Caroline tried to keep her breaths nice and even. She would have preferred to choose her own table, but obviously that wasn't going to happen. *It's not a big deal,* Caroline told herself. *Everyone here is an artist. They must be okay.*

Setting aside Lara's warnings about the existence of jerk-ish kids, Caroline slid into an empty seat. She smiled at the other kids at the table. The boy sitting next to her was already scribbling a comic-style fight scene on notebook paper.

"Welcome to Experimental Art! Don't worry—we will definitely be making art today," the teacher said. "But first things first! I'd love for us to get to know each other better. Let's take some time for you guys to talk with everyone else at your table."

Caroline drew in a breath and pulled out her tablet. Okay. She could totally do this. She opened the speech app and readied her fingers for typing.

"What are we supposed to be talking about?" the boy wondered. He was still working away on his comic.

"It would help to know your name, genius," said a red-haired girl with a tight ponytail. "I'll start. I'm Marissa and I'm a painter. My favorite medium is acrylics and I went to art camp this summer. I won an award for best portrait."

Caroline gulped. She knew art wasn't a competition, exactly, but the idea of being in the same class as braggy Marissa made her nervous.

"I'm more into watercolors," another girl said. "Oh, yeah. I'm Jenna. Hi and nice to meet you."

Although Caroline couldn't quite bring herself to look Jenna in the eyes, her shoulders relaxed. At least Jenna seemed nice.

"How about you?" Jenna asked the boy.

He looked up from his drawing. "Micah. I like comics, obviously."

Marissa looked at his work and sniffed. "You're not bad. Why don't you do real art?"

"Comics is real art!"

"If you say so."

Caroline sensed that this argument could go on for the rest of class if left unchecked. She decided to intervene. With a quick tap to her tablet, she said her introduction: "Hello! My name is Caroline Finkel. I am eleven years old and I like art. It is nice to meet you."

The rest of the Blue Table stared. Marissa's mouth

hung open into a rather unbecoming O-shape. "Oh," she said. "So that's how you . . . talk."

Caroline did not like the pause in Marissa's voice. As though Caroline's way of talking was somehow less real than anyone else's. As though Caroline herself was less real.

She decided that Marissa's meanness deserved only a one-word response: "Yes."

Apparently, Marissa decided that Caroline didn't warrant any further attention, because she turned back to the other kids and started talking about her recent trip to Paris, which she pronounced as "Par-ee" for some reason. That was more than okay with Caroline. She switched over to Candy Crush on her tablet and restarted level 457. Technically she wasn't supposed to use her tablet for games during school, but it's not as if they were doing anything actually important. Next to her, Micah continued his drawing. Caroline was tempted to take a peek, but resisted the urge. She never liked to show her work before it was done, so it was hardly fair to look at someone else's.

"Now it's time for your very first project!" the pink-haired woman announced. Caroline realized she should probably figure out her real name. "I don't want to give you any restrictions, except for this: I would like for all of you to work in a medium that you've never used before. This is a chance for you to experiment and grow as artists. We are in Experimental Art, after all!"

Marissa immediately raised her hand to announce that she was familiar with all possible mediums. While she babbled on, Caroline considered her options. The idea of using a new medium excited her—but what should she choose?

Her gaze was instantly drawn to the heaps of red-brown clay sitting in plastic bags. She certainly didn't have much experience with that. Before she could think about it too much, Caroline wandered over to the clay and grabbed a bag for herself.

She ripped the bag open and stared at the clay for a good minute or so before scooping out a nice big chunk. This clay could become so many different things, but what would be the very best?

After rolling the clay into a perfectly even ball, Caroline paused. She had no idea what to do next. Caroline was just about ready to flatten the ball into a pancake when the teacher strolled up. "Excellent choice of medium. Do you know what you're sculpting?"

Her tablet was close enough, but Caroline didn't want

to risk messing it up with clay-coated fingers. She shook her head.

"It's totally okay not to know right away. You want to let the clay guide you." She handed Caroline a set of tools. "This will help."

Even though Caroline did not have the first clue about how to let the clay guide her toward anything but a colossally ugly mess, she nodded.

She set the clay on the table and started to shape it with her bare hands. Much to her surprise, a form started to emerge. Caroline thought the clay looked a little like a horse's head. But horses were quite boring. She needed a more interesting animal that looked kind of like a horse. Thinking back to family trips to the Woodland Park Zoo, she decided that the sculpture would be a zebra. Yes, that was good. And half an hour into class, her clay was clearly recognizable as a zebra's head.

Bit by bit, the zebra came to life. Caroline decided she ought to have a name. Helena seemed like a good choice. Thanks to Caroline's hands, Helena soon grew oval-shaped ears, wide nostrils, and clay eyes that watched Caroline as she worked.

"This is excellent work!" the teacher told her. "Are you sure you've never worked with clay before?"

Caroline shook her head. She'd worked on a potter's wheel once or twice in elementary school, but she'd certainly never sculpted like this before.

"Well, you're a natural sculptor. I'm super impressed."

Caroline would be lying if she said that the praise didn't make her want to jump up and down. Maybe she did belong here at Pinecone Arts Academy.

She continued to define Helena's features, a silly grin firmly attached to her face. She paused only upon realizing that she really, really had to go to the bathroom. She didn't want to abandon her work, but even great artists had to go sometimes, surely.

When she returned, Helena was gone.

No. That wasn't quite accurate. Helena wasn't gone. Her basic form was still there—the head, the neck, the ears. But otherwise, she had been completely destroyed.

A strangled cry escaped from Caroline's throat.

The other kids' eyes bored into her, and Caroline wished she could somehow shoo them all away. She rocked back and forth, trying and failing to calm the screaming in her brain.

For once she didn't see any colors. Just blank canvas.

"Oh, no!" the teacher exclaimed. "I was checking up on some of our other artists and . . . oh, no."

She narrowed her eyes and looked over the room of kids, with an expression far grimmer than Caroline would have believed possible for someone with pink hair. "Now. Does anyone know what happened to Caroline's sculpture?"

Silence descended upon the room for one long and horrible moment. Then two. Then . . .

"She did it!"

Micah pointed his finger right at Marissa.

The teacher frowned and turned toward them. "Is this true?"

Caroline did not listen to Marissa's rapid stream of words, which became increasingly high-pitched. All she could hear was the scream in her own mind.

She'd been so close to making something beautiful. Now, thanks to a stupid trip to the bathroom, it was all gone and she could never, ever bring it back.

With any luck, she wouldn't have any more classes with Marissa. But that didn't really matter, did it? Lara had been right: Middle school was full of jerks. There would always be Marissas, in this class and in every other one she attended.

How could she possibly make it through the entire school year here?

CHAPTER TEN:

OF NEW FRIENDS
AND OLD SISTERS

Caroline would have preferred for her school day to end right then and there, but of course it didn't. She still had a whole list of classes to suffer through before she could go home and bury herself in her comforter. Next up was math, which had never been one of her favorite subjects.

Tears pushed against Caroline's eyes for the entire class period. She didn't actually cry, thank goodness, but the threat of it felt far too present. Not crying took up so much of her concentration, in fact, that she failed to understand a single word that the teacher said.

". . . finish that for tomorrow," the teacher said at the end of class.

Caroline flinched. Well, there was yet another thing for her to fail at. Unless she could ask someone about the assignment. At elementary school, she could have always asked her paraprofessional about it later. But things were different here, in this strange place where they changed classes every hour. Here there was no paraprofessional, and she didn't know anyone else. Not really.

It took Caroline thirty whole seconds to realize that it was now time to go. Gathering up her things didn't take much time, since she hadn't bothered taking out her notebook in the first place.

"Hey," a voice came from behind her.

She swung around to face a dark-haired boy with thick glasses. She had seen him before, probably, but she could not quite place him. Remembering faces could be hard for Caroline. Hopefully, he would not be terribly offended by her failure to recognize him.

Her tablet was still around her neck, but since she didn't much care for talking and walking at the same time, she just nodded.

"Pretty boring class, right?"

Caroline nodded again. She was a little surprised that the boy kept talking to her. In Caroline's considerable experience, most people had little interest in continuing a conversation with someone who didn't talk back right away. Clearly, this boy was not most people.

"Um . . . I hope it's not rude or whatever to say this, but are you okay?"

After the morning's events, Caroline felt very not-okay.

Weirdly enough, this boy asking her about it made her feel a tiny bit more okay.

"It's cool if you don't want to talk right now. If you actually hate talking to me, you can totally leave. I don't want to bore you to death when you're already having a bad day."

Caroline continued to match her stride to the boy's quick steps. Upon taking another look at him, she realized why he was so familiar. It was Micah, the boy from art class. Without a pencil in his hand, it had been difficult to recognize him at first.

"Oh, so you like talking to me?" Micah said. "Cool. So I just wanted to tell you that I thought the zebra was awesome. And Marissa is totally the worst. After that she deserves a little payback, if you ask me."

The idea of payback felt ominous to Caroline. But she had to admit that there was definitely some appeal.

"You're not the only one, you know. Marissa and her friends went to the same elementary school as me last year. They probably made half the fifth-grade class cry at one point. Including, well, me."

Caroline gave Micah what she could only hope was a sympathetic smile. She wondered what Marissa could have done to make him cry, but it didn't seem polite to ask.

"This is, um, kind of embarrassing to admit, but she told

everyone that I peed my pants. I didn't! Everyone called me Micah Pee from then on—you know, because my last name is Perkowski. Anyway. I just wanted to tell you that you're not alone. I'll stop talking if you want now."

Biting her lip, Caroline tried to figure out how to tell the boy that yes, he could keep on talking to her. She settled on shaking her head, giving him a big smile.

"Really? You don't mind me going on like this? Wow. I think you might be the only one."

Grinning widely, Micah patted her on the back. Caroline didn't much like being touched, but she appreciated the effort.

"I'm going to lunch. You want to sit together?"

Never before had Caroline nodded quite so quickly.

✳ ✳ ✳

LOCATION: Language arts class, fourth period

EVENT: Nothing, nothing, and more nothing. At least as far as I know.

QUESTION FOR FURTHER INVESTIGATION: How is C. doing?

Lara tried not to worry about how Caroline's day was going. After all, there were plenty of other things to worry about: her gym teacher's promise that they'd be running the mile by the end of the week. The fact that her creative writing teacher spent twenty minutes talking about her high expectations. The early beginnings of a headache bubbling just behind her temples.

Still, as she went about her own first day, she couldn't help but wonder what Caroline was doing just a few hallways over.

Surely nothing too bad could have happened. If it did, Lara would know.

Except that she didn't.

The very worst happened in fourth period, just after lunch. In the middle of an admittedly dull getting-to-know-you exercise, Lara's language arts teacher came over to her table. "The principal wants to speak with you," the teacher told Lara.

Lara gulped. Her first thought was that she could not possibly be in trouble after half a day of school. Surely.

Her second thought was that something must have happened to Caroline.

Lara ran to Principal Jenkins's office with far more speed than her usual gym-class jog. By the time she arrived at the office, she was panting.

Caroline was there, looking perfectly miserable as she stared at her tablet screen.

"Hi," she said to Lara.

"What happened?" Lara said. There was no time for hellos.

It became immediately clear that Caroline did not want to answer the question. Principal Jenkins sighed. "Maybe you'd better sit down."

Lara sat.

"I'm sorry I didn't call you girls in earlier," the principal began. "I was in meetings all morning and only just found out about this."

"Can you just tell me what happened?" Lara blurted out.

"I'm getting to that."

Principal Jenkins kept her voice level as she explained what had happened. Lara's nerves made it difficult to catch every detail, but what she did hear was more than enough to send her into an epic rage. Apparently, some girl had destroyed Caroline's sculpture. Lara would have liked to go charging into every sixth-grade classroom in the school. She wanted to find this girl and give her a proper scolding. But that didn't seem like a very practical idea, at least not right now. It was definitely something for future consideration, though.

"Is she being punished?" Lara demanded once the talking appeared to be done.

The principal frowned. "Yes. But that's not your concern. I did not invite you here to discuss another student's discipline. I wanted you to help your sister."

Right. That probably was the most important thing right now. Lara turned to Caroline. "Are you okay? Do we need to call Dad and Ima?"

"No," Caroline said. It was the first word she'd said throughout the whole thing. "I'm okay. I just want to go back to class."

Biting her lip, Lara looked over at her sister. She knew—she just knew—when Caroline was or was not okay. And she was pretty sure that Caroline was not okay.

Principal Jenkins sighed. Then she nodded. "If that's what you want, then I will respect that. Although I should let you know that I have left a message on your father's voicemail explaining the situation."

Lara almost snorted. She wanted to say that there was no chance at all that Dad would listen to the message within the next two months. But Caroline elbowed her, and Lara knew that was her cue to keep quiet.

"I am sorry this happened on your first day," Principal Jenkins said. "This is not the kind of behavior we approve of at Pinecone Arts Academy."

Caroline squirmed in her seat. "Can I go now?"

Another loud-enough-to-hear sigh came from Principal Jenkins. "Yes, you may go. You too," she said, looking at Lara.

Lara leaped to her feet. But she still wasn't fast enough to catch up with Caroline.

Scowling, she returned to language arts class. As everyone else began to make posters about their summer reading, Lara pulled out her detective notebook. She didn't even try to be sneaky.

PROBLEM: Caroline doesn't want to talk with me. For some reason.

CHAPTER ELEVEN:

SECRET MESSAGES

By the end of her first day, Caroline could only feel anger. The problem began with Marissa, though it did not end there. Perhaps it wasn't 100 percent reasonable of her, but Caroline was mad at Lara and Principal Jenkins, too. Why did everyone think she needed help, that she couldn't handle her own problems?

After all, she'd been dealing with Marissas her entire life. Maybe Marissa was worse than most, but even so. Caroline could handle it on her own, thank you very much.

As soon as Lara met her after school, Caroline issued a warning: "Don't tell Dad what happened."

Just as Caroline expected, her sister frowned. "He should know! Besides, Principal Jenkins left a message on his phone."

Caroline gave Lara a look that hopefully communicated "will you stop being ridiculous please." Only maybe she didn't need the *please* part. "Dad is not going to check his messages. Don't you think he has enough to deal with right now?"

Lara made a face, but Caroline could tell her argument had worked. Good.

"I still think Dad and Ima should know," Lara said after a pause. "But if you really don't want me to tell . . ."

Her voice trailed off—a decidedly unusual occurrence for Lara. Caroline took advantage of the opportunity and typed at top speed. "Promise me you won't tell."

Although her lips were still in pout position, Lara nodded. "I won't tell. But you have to promise me something, too."

"Okay." Caroline didn't like it, but she was hardly in a position to refuse.

"Promise me that you'll let me know if Marissa tries anything again."

Caroline tapped the "yes" button and ignored the twinge in her stomach. Because, of course, she had no intention of telling Lara anything about Marissa.

It felt strange. For so long Lara had been Caroline's person. But things were different now, weren't they? Caroline wanted to be her own person, not Lara's sidekick.

Still, Caroline continued to feel not-quite-right as Dad picked them up from school and as they began their homework. Lara felt far away, even though she was just on the other side of the bedroom.

Just before dinner, Caroline's phone pinged. She had a text from an unfamiliar number:

Hey

She frowned. Caroline didn't usually get many text messages, except boring ones from her family. Benny had a habit of sharing GIFs of aardvarks drinking pop and whatnot. She tapped out a quick response to the mystery texter.

Who are you?

Moments later, an answer appeared.

Micah

Caroline smiled at the name and happy blue paint streaks took shape. Of course! She'd given her phone number to Micah during lunch. Twirling her hair, she thought about what to say back. It occurred to her that texting was similar to her speech app. She liked that.

Another text popped up while Caroline considered her options.

So what are you doing?

Not much. Homework.
How about you?

That sounded sufficiently friend-like, Caroline thought.

Same. Why do they assign homework
on the first day?

I guess that's just middle school.

Yeah.

The creak of a door forced Caroline's attention away from her phone. She glanced up to see Dad shuffle in. Noting his messy curls and stained T-shirt, Caroline frowned.

"Hey," Dad said.

She tried to push aside her worries and smile at him. "Hi. I'm texting with my new friend."

Caroline pointed to her phone.

"That's great, honey," Dad said. But Caroline thought he didn't sound properly enthusiastic.

"Yep," Caroline replied.

Dad darted his eyes around the room, looking a little like Kugel did when he chased his laser toy. "You haven't happened to see your mother's brooch around here recently?"

"No," Caroline replied immediately. The only place she'd seen one of Ima's brooches was on Ima, and even that was quite rare. Her mother didn't usually wear jewelry.

Her father sighed. "Well, keep an eye out for it, okay? Ima's family brought it over from Turkey and it's really important to her. Turquoise and silver, two or three inches wide."

"Sure," Caroline said, only half paying attention.

Caroline glanced back at her phone. While she'd been talking to Dad, Micah had typed out several additional messages.

So I've been thinking

What Marissa did to you wasn't cool

At all

We should do something

Payback

For several minutes, Caroline just stared at her screen. She certainly couldn't disagree about the uncoolness of Marissa's actions. But the whole idea of payback just made her feel a little funny in her stomach.

What do you mean?

You'll see.

*It's better to talk about that
in person.*

*Ok. I'm excited to hear
about it.*

But as she stared at Micah's words, Caroline felt no excitement whatsoever.

CHAPTER TWELVE:

THE UNEXPECTED ADVENTURE

Given the not-good-ness of Caroline's first day at middle school, she was rather surprised to find that the next few days were very good indeed.

She certainly had not anticipated that she would enjoy lunch at Pinecone Arts Academy. Yet she did, and it was all thanks to Micah.

They had their usual table—in the corner, where it was less noisy. Caroline was pretty sure Micah had deliberately chosen the table after she mentioned how much she hated all the clanging and chatter in the cafeteria.

The food itself wasn't anything special. Dad's culinary creativity appeared to have abandoned him, and Caroline found herself eating quite a few roast beef sandwiches—extra cheese, no tomato. But that was okay. Lunch wasn't about the food.

Caroline had gotten into the habit of holding her sandwich in one hand while she tapped on her phone with the other. She and Micah had a constant stream of text messages going, and lunchtime was their busiest time.

Even though she'd told Micah, on numerous occasions, that he could speak out loud to her if he wanted, he said he liked the idea of texting better. *Way cooler*, he'd texted. *Plus we have privacy. Nosy people can't overhear us.*

In truth Caroline did not have the slightest idea why anyone would want to listen in on their conversations about Micah's comic project and her opinions on the best brand of colored pencils. But she liked the idea that Micah wanted to keep their conversations private.

A text from Micah lit up her phone.

I like your giraffe.

The compliment brought an immediate smile to her face. After the disaster with her zebra, Caroline had begun another sculpture in art class. Ms. Williamson praised it, filling Caroline with a warm glow despite her lingering fear that someone might destroy her work at any moment.

Thanks

Why haven't you made another zebra?

Caroline bit her lip. She had not forgotten Micah's promise that Marissa would pay for what she'd done. Now she had to nudge him away from the topic, and quickly.

Just didn't want to.
Maybe another time.

I have an idea.

And there it was. Caroline's heartbeat quickened as she rapidly typed out a response.

About what?

Marissa.

We should pull a prank on her. I'm still working on the details, but I have an idea. Just wait till you hear it.

If it had been Lara who had proposed a revenge plot, Caroline would have had no problem telling her exactly what she thought about it. But Micah wasn't Lara. He must have loads of other kids who wanted to be his friend, surely.

Several minutes passed while Caroline stared at her screen. She had to say something, she knew.

Frowning, Caroline settled on:

Are you sure?

Micah's response was swift.

Yep. Don't worry. We won't do anything that really hurts her. My brothers and I play pranks on each other all the time.

Caroline chewed on her lip and considered her options. Ima sometimes gave her advice on talking to people. One of Ima's best tips was, *If someone is talking about something you don't want to discuss, just change the subject.* It was one of her favorite ways to handle Lara when she got particularly annoying. Maybe it could work with Micah, too.

> *How many brothers do*
> *you have?*

Two. I'm the youngest.

Caroline smiled at the response and quickly composed her own.

> *I'm second-youngest.*
> *Two brothers and a sister.*

So you get all of the youngest
child problems.

When they say "you'll understand when
you're older," isn't that the WORST?
And they keep saying it, even when
we get older too!

> *Definitely! Noah always says*
> *that. And my sister is really,*
> *really bossy. She thinks being*
> *a year older means she gets*
> *to be in charge of everything.*

Caroline felt a little bad about calling Lara bossy behind her back, but it was true. Besides, she had steered

Micah away from the subject of Marissa. That was a success of sorts.

Yeah, that sounds like my brothers.
Plus, they use me as the guinea pig for
their pranks. So I learned to fight back.

No, no, no. That was not the way Caroline wanted this conversation to go. She searched for a good reply—something that would make Micah forget all about pranks and revenge and other dangerous subjects. But she was too late. Micah continued typing.

That's how I learned to do pranks.
So don't worry, I'm totally an expert.

We can do something to Marissa.
She deserves it.

It's fun. You'll see.

Clenching her arms around her chest, Caroline racked her brain for an objection. Something that didn't sound even a little bit cowardly. Maybe she could . . .

But before Caroline decided on a course of action, something hard hit the back of her head. By reflex, she jumped to her feet and let out a yelp. Her entire body vibrated, and Caroline needed to use all of her energy to keep herself from screaming. No matter how very much she wanted to scream, she couldn't. Not in front of the entire sixth grade, with Micah sitting right there.

"Sorry, man! I missed," said a tall boy who came up from behind. "I meant to throw it at my jerk of a friend over there."

Caroline had no idea why one would want to throw something at a friend, but she supposed that wasn't really her business. The boy retrieved the unwelcome projectile—a pear, as it turned out—from the floor. To Caroline's disgust, he looked as though he might still eat it.

Under the circumstances, she could not even think about typing out a reply. She tried to do the deep-breathing exercises her therapist recommended for situations such as these, but all the commotion in the cafeteria made it difficult to concentrate on counting the inhales and exhales.

The boy looked at her strangely, but did not comment any further. Caroline wondered if she was already known throughout the sixth grade as The Girl Who Doesn't Speak.

Micah sprang into action, giving the other boy a fierce glare. Caroline felt very, very glad that this glare had not yet been directed at her.

"Well, try and watch where you throw your lunch from now on," Micah said. " 'Kay?"

"You got it." The boy turned to Caroline again. "I really am sorry."

Caroline nodded and forced herself back into her chair. She managed one big deep breath, then two and three. By breath number eight she felt okay, or at least most of the way there.

Micah smiled at her and a burst of affection swelled within her chest. Grinning broadly, she turned back to her phone and once again opened their text thread.

Thanks.

Caroline's fingers hovered over the keys as she considered what to type next. There was so much more she could say. Thanks for defending me. Thanks for not freaking out when I freaked out. Thanks for not making a big deal over everything now.

But Caroline wasn't quite sure how to say any of that without sounding, well, kind of uncool. So she pressed the "send" button, hoping that her single word would somehow communicate everything she really wanted to say.

Micah's response came back almost instantaneously.

No prob.

Caroline flashed him a thumbs-up and started eating her sandwich again. Somehow it tasted better than before.

While she ate, Micah took out his sketchbook and worked on his comic strip. He didn't say anything else about Marissa and his plan for the rest of the lunch period.

Still, Caroline thought about it. Micah was an awfully good friend to her. Would it really be so bad to play one teeny-tiny prank?

Yes! Caroline's conscience screamed.

But another part of her whispered, *Maybe not.*

By the end of the day, Caroline's mood was frayed. To make matters even worse, Dad hadn't shown up, twenty-two full minutes after the end of school.

"Is there some reason why Dad might be late?" Caroline asked her sister as they waited with Aviva by the main entrance.

Some part of Caroline wanted to believe that Dad had just been held up by a super-important meeting. Some adult thing he absolutely could not get out of, no matter how much he wanted to.

Because surely her father would come pick them up if he could, wouldn't he?

"Well, you know Dad," Lara said finally. As if that were a real answer.

A few feet away, Aviva shifted from foot to foot in a jittery dance. That only had the effect of increasing Caroline's nerves. She could tell it made Lara anxious too, but surprisingly, she didn't say anything about it.

"Let me text him," Lara said, eyes fixed on her glowing phone screen.

Aviva added a hand-flap to her dance, and Caroline smiled in spite of the uncertainty. She always found it comforting to see her movements, so often mocked by other kids, in other people. In that way she was definitely lucky to have her family. As far as Caroline could tell, *not* being autistic or having ADHD was weird for the Rosanes-Finkel family. Maybe Noah felt left out sometimes. He was the only Finkel sibling that was remotely normal—whatever *normal* meant.

As the minutes passed, Aviva's flapping and pacing sped up. Caroline started flapping herself, and she could tell that Lara was ready to join them soon. Her sister's hand seemingly had not strayed from the phone for five minutes straight.

"Did you try texting Dad again?" Caroline asked. Maybe he'd missed the ping of his phone the first time.

"Of course I did," Lara replied. The tension in her voice

made Caroline flinch. "I've texted him six times since we've been here. Right now I'm working on number seven."

Aviva, still pacing on the sidewalk, spoke. "Maybe he is busy at work."

"That's not possible," Caroline said.

She realized her mistake the moment she tapped "speak" on her app. Aviva stopped pacing and stared.

Arms crossed over her chest, Lara looked at Caroline. "Our dad lost his job," she said flatly.

Her cousin frowned. "I do not understand," she said. "Why does your dad losing his job mean he cannot pick us up?"

It was an entirely reasonable question, and one that Caroline couldn't begin to answer adequately. Fortunately, Lara had a response as always.

"That is very complicated."

"Complicated how?" A crease appeared on Aviva's brow.

"You wouldn't understand," Lara said, in a tone that made Caroline wince. "You don't know Dad like we do. Sorry."

Lara did not sound very sorry.

Aviva didn't say anything more, but Caroline was thoroughly annoyed with her sister. She searched her brain for the right words to express her displeasure at Lara's meanness and began to tap at her tablet. She was nearly ready to press "speak" on her rant when Lara spoke again. This time her voice was light and airy.

"Well, I don't think Dad is coming. But that's okay. We can just get home ourselves. I have enough emergency money for the bus."

Aviva's hands began to flap at least 10 percent faster than before in Caroline's estimation. "The bus?" she repeated. "Are we allowed to do that?"

"I've done it before," Lara said, which wasn't exactly an answer to the question that had been asked.

While Lara explained, in her most annoying Big Sister voice, how taking the bus home was totally the easiest thing in the history of ever, Caroline composed a new paragraph on her tablet. It was full of rational points about how they should simply try to contact their parents again rather than attempt something that was sure to go wrong. Something that was most certainly Against the Rules.

Of course Lara only rolled her eyes at Caroline's well-considered points. "Lina-Lin, don't worry so much. The bus will get us home in no time. And Dad and Ima can't very well get mad at us, since Dad didn't pick us up in the first place."

"We should at least try calling Ima first," Caroline said, although she could tell she was on the very edge of losing the argument.

"I already texted her twice. She hasn't responded. She's probably busy delivering a baby or doing another doctorly thing." Lara made a face. "Come on. You guys aren't afraid of going on the bus, are you?"

"Of course not," Aviva said quickly. Caroline shook her head, even though she was still convinced it was all a terrible idea.

And so when Lara marched toward the bus stop, Caroline followed a mere half step behind.

CHAPTER THIRTEEN:

A MOST UNUSUAL SIGHTING

LOCATION: *Outside of Pinecone Arts Academy, 3:00 p.m.*

EVENT: *Dad doesn't pick us up from school.*

QUESTION FOR FURTHER INVESTIGATION: *Has he for-gotten about us?*

Lara peered out the bus window, fingers flapping lightly against her jeans. She wasn't about to admit it to Caroline and Aviva, but she didn't feel completely sure they'd gotten on the right bus. She was more like mostly sure. Okay, mostly-ish.

Caroline tapped Lara on the shoulder for about the twelfth time in as many minutes. She didn't have her speech app open, since she was currently engrossed in doing something on her phone, but Lara understood the gesture's meaning perfectly.

"Yes, we're on the right bus," Lara said for the twelfth time. "Trust me."

In a seat across from them, Aviva swung her legs back

and forth. She kept flitting her gaze about, as though someone might descend at any moment to catch them riding the bus without permission.

"Don't you have buses in Israel?" Lara asked, irked by Aviva's skittishness.

Aviva straightened her back and stopped swinging. "Certainly," she said. "Although they usually smell better than this."

"Of course they do," Lara muttered. She didn't bother resisting the impulse to roll her eyes.

"This bus is going to take us home, right?" Aviva asked.

"For the millionth time, yes. I'm sure of it," Lara said. It was only a tiny lie. Hardly a lie at all, really. "I've taken the bus home from school before."

She very purposefully did not mention that the scenes rolling past in the windows didn't feel quite right to her. After all, it had been months since she'd last taken the bus. In another few minutes she'd start to see more familiar sights—the park in the Finkels' neighborhood, the Dairy Queen they sometimes visited together. She just had to wait a little.

The bus lurched to a stop. Lara groaned when she spotted a horde of people entering. They looked like high school kids, and while Lara generally didn't mind high schoolers, high school kids on the bus was another matter altogether. In Lara's experience, they tended to be even louder than most other bus riders. The presence of a whole group of them was sure to generate a truly unbearable level of noise.

Lara flapped her hands a bit harder as the group invaded the bus. She soon found herself staring at a purple backpack just inches from her face. Ugh—why did high school kids have to carry such enormous bags all the time?

After the bus made a few stops, the crowd thinned and Lara found it easier to breathe. She glanced out the window again, hoping to catch sight of a landmark she recognized.

Instead, she was met with a very familiar face reflected in the glass.

"Noah!" Lara blurted out. "What are you doing here?"

Lara stared at her brother. He stared back. Noah didn't seem particularly surprised to see her, and she wondered if he'd spotted her first. Why hadn't he said hi?

"What are you doing here?" she asked.

He gave a slight smile. "I could ask you the same question. I probably should, being the older brother and all."

"We are going home from school," Lara informed him. He didn't really need to know anything more than that.

Noah's eyebrows shot upward. "Really? Are you sure about that?"

"Yes. Why?" Lara could feel Caroline's shoulder muscles clench up. Her sister had stopped the constant tapping on her phone.

"Well, this bus doesn't go anywhere near our house," Noah said.

"What? I thought the 745 stopped on our street!"

Caroline glared, and Lara could just hear her saying "I told you so."

"Yeah, the 745 does go by our house. But you want the bus going in the other direction. This bus will take you to Bothell if you stay on long enough," Noah said. "I'm gonna take a wild guess and say you don't want to go there."

A heavy flush spread itself all over Lara's face and neck. It was, she had to admit, kind of an embarrassing mistake. Both Caroline and Aviva looked most displeased. Lara couldn't really blame them. She struggled to keep calm.

"Okay, so I made a little mistake. But it's easy enough to fix it. We just get off at the next stop, cross the street, and get on the other bus. Right?"

Lara wished she could take back the shakiness that crept into her voice as she laid out the new plan.

Noah nodded. "Yeah, that's definitely what you

should do. Only . . . are you guys okay? Why isn't Dad picking you up?"

"He wanted me to show Lina-Lin and Aviva how to take the bus," Lara said. Her stomach squirmed at the lie. "And it's definitely been an adventure, hasn't it?"

A sharp poke from Caroline told Lara everything she needed to know about her sister's opinion on the matter.

Noah opened his mouth to say more, but the sudden jerk of the bus prevented Lara from paying attention to whatever it was he had to say. She grabbed Caroline's hand and leaped up from her seat. "Come on. We need to get off now."

Lara supposed she should be grateful that the other two followed her without further comment.

As they waited for another bus to come around—the correct one, hopefully—a pressing question started to nag Lara. If the bus didn't go to the Finkels' house, then why was Noah still riding it?

Somehow, they made it back to the Finkel house without any further incident. Lara felt a burst of pride when she rounded the corner and saw that familiar yellow door. From the exhaustion drooping all over Caroline's face, Lara knew better than to say "See! I told you I could get us home!"

But she certainly thought it.

Her next task was decidedly less pleasant, though she just didn't see any way around it. Lara needed to talk with Dad.

He was in his office, of course. The door was completely closed, and Lara could hear the faintly tapping symphony of his keyboard. She tried to tell herself that he was typing very important things, things that would help him get a new job. Still, that didn't change the basic facts. Dad had forgotten them.

Lara opened the door. Knocking seemed rather unnecessary. Her father's head jerked toward the door immediately, and the moment he saw her, his mouth fell into a grimace. "L-Lara! Gosh, I'm so sorry . . . I must have lost track of time."

"It's okay," Lara told him, even though it wasn't. "We got home fine. We just went on the bus."

"Good, good." Dad's expression still spoke plainly of discomfort. "But . . . Benny!"

It took a moment for Lara to catch her father's meaning, but when she did, her face paled several shades. Benny! Was he still standing in front of his elementary school, waiting for a ride home that wouldn't come?

Then she remembered and the fear went away. "It's

Tuesday. He goes over to his friend's house on Tuesday and they work on robotics projects."

"Right, of course." Dad let out a breath loud enough to hear even over the laptop's humming fan. "That was some smart thinking with the bus. I really don't know how to tell you how sorry I am, Lara-bear. I know it's a bogus excuse, but I was really busy working. I just got caught up in things and it completely slipped my mind that it was time to go pick you guys up."

Lara's skin felt as though she'd stumbled into a bathtub full of hot needles. She hadn't really been mad at her father for forgetting to pick them up. Not really. But now, listening to the humongous lie, she felt very angry indeed.

"I know you lost your job," Lara told him. Her voice trembled, which probably meant that she ought to stop talking, at least for a bit. She kept at it anyway. "Stop lying to me! I know you weren't working! You were just here, doing . . . I don't even know what you could have been doing."

Lara's skin prickled as she waited to hear what her father was going to say. For a very long time, he didn't say anything at all.

She could imagine what he must be thinking. Mind

your own business, Lara. Stop being so annoying, Lara. Leave things to the adults, Lara.

Dad didn't say any of those things. When the silence finally came to an end, a single word came out. "Yes."

Lara wished he would have told her off. She wished he would have done anything except just sit there, silent and still aside from the nervous twitching in his fingers.

"Do your siblings know?" he asked after another heavy silence.

"Caroline does," Lara replied. "So does Aviva."

Dad exhaled and nodded. "Please don't tell anyone else. I don't want to worry them. I'm going to find another job really soon."

An alarming thought entered her mind. "Does . . . does Ima know?" she asked.

"Of course she does." Dad looked bewildered at the question, and Lara allowed herself a small sigh of relief. "So does your aunt Miriam, of course. We just thought it would be best not to worry you kids."

Lara thought back to Aviva's anxious pacing when Dad failed to show up this afternoon. To Caroline's nervous fidgets. She couldn't help but think the grown-ups had done a very poor job of not worrying the rest of them.

She considered saying so, but one look at her father's

face made her think better of it. "Okay," she mumbled.

"Thanks, Lara-bear." At long last, Dad's face relaxed into something that resembled his typical expression. "I really am so sorry that I missed picking you guys up. It won't happen again. I promise."

"Okay," Lara repeated.

Yet she wasn't sure she believed him.

CHAPTER FOURTEEN:

THE CASE OF THE WEIRD PARENTS

LOCATION: House, 4:30 p.m.

*EVENT: Talked to Dad. He admitted that he lost his job.
Finally.*

*QUESTION FOR FURTHER INVESTIGATION: Why does one
bad thing happening mean that everything else falls apart?*

Lara definitely did not continue to dwell on the afternoon's events. No, she put every effort toward doing
other things. Math homework, reading her favorite Georgia Ketteridge fan pages, and even a little bat mitzvah
prep. (Very little, if she was being honest.)

After staring at the same Hebrew word for five minutes, Lara had to admit that maybe she really was thinking about Dad and his troubles.

She needed a true distraction. So she marched upstairs
to the bedroom, where she found Caroline sprawled
across the bed, eyes fixed to her phone screen.

Lara frowned. This sight had become quite common

in the Finkel household—perhaps too common. Who was Caroline texting? Whenever Lara asked, her sister replied "a friend." Like that was somehow informative.

When Caroline caught sight of her sister, she made a face and shoved the phone underneath a pillow. As if she was afraid that Lara could somehow see it from seven feet away. The whole thing was so bizarre, it made Lara want to read her sister's texts even more.

Maybe she could concoct some kind of a plan to tear Caroline away from the phone so she could take a little peek. Just to check up on her sister and make sure she wasn't in trouble. True, Lara couldn't imagine what Caroline of all people could possibly be doing to make trouble. But there was no harm in checking, was there? It was practically her duty as the big sister.

She just needed to do something. It had to be big enough to draw Caroline away from the room without the phone. Maybe . . .

The sound of very angry voices pierced through the hallway. Lara's body jerked.

Instinct prompted her to glance over at her sister right away. A frown-shaped wrinkle popped up on Caroline's forehead. Lara's own mouth drew into a matching frown at the sight.

"It's Dad and Ima," Lara whispered.

"I know," Caroline said, switching over to her tablet quickly.

Even though Caroline soon turned back to her phone, Lara knew her sister was bothered by the ever-louder noises coming from down the hall. How could she not be?

One minute passed, then two. The voices continued, and Lara's heart started thumping at an alarming rate.

This kind of thing just didn't happen. Not to Dad and Ima. Lara wouldn't have believed it was happening, except for the simple, undeniable fact that it *was* happening.

She needed to do something. Lara nodded at her sister. "Let's go."

Caroline didn't question it. She just clutched her tablet to her chest and joined Lara.

It was time to do some investigating. Even if Lara wasn't quite sure she wanted to know the conclusions of this particular investigation.

Lara did her very best to keep quiet while she tiptoed down the hall. As she and Caroline drew closer to the master bedroom, Ima's voice got louder.

Lara's heartbeat quickened further, reverberating throughout her entire body. Trying to ignore the unpleasantness, she crouched by the closed door. She didn't care about not looking suspicious. She needed to hear every single word. Once her left ear brushed up against the wooden door, she stopped moving. Next to her, Caroline did the same.

". . . yes, now Lara knows," Dad was saying. His voice hadn't yet reached Ima levels, but the note of annoyance punctuating his words could hardly be missed.

"I cannot believe you forgot to pick the children up from school," Ima told him. Even on the other side of the door, Lara could feel angry vibrations radiating from her mother.

"I don't know how many ways I can possibly tell you that I feel terrible and it won't happen again. I promise."

The responding sniff caused Lara to wince. "Your feeling terrible does not change the fact that our children—and my sister's child too—could have been badly hurt as the result of your negligence."

"Oh, come on." Dad's voice jumped to a higher pitch. "I messed up, but you're exaggerating. They were fine. Lara's smart. She can take care of things okay."

Normally such a compliment would have made Lara glow. Instead, she just felt . . . she didn't even know what she felt.

"Anyway, none of this is going to matter," Dad continued. "I'm going to find a new job and everything will be good again."

"Will you?"

Ima's voice was almost too quiet to hear. As Lara registered her mother's meaning, she let out a cry against her will.

Surely such a sound would prompt Dad and Ima to leave their room, finally. Lara almost would have welcomed the discovery.

No one came.

"Well, what's that supposed to mean?" Dad asked finally.

For a long time, Ima did not say another word. Lara could hear her own heartbeat trying to escape the confines of her chest, and she felt sure that Dad and Ima could hear it too.

Another glance over at Caroline revealed a stream of tears running down her cheeks.

Ima let out a long exhale. The air itself almost seemed to hiss.

"I don't want to argue with you," she said. "I just want to solve the problem so we can move on with our lives."

"I told you. I've got this under control. I'm applying for jobs. I'll get one of them. Everything will work out. And then we can move on with our lives."

Funny, how different the words sounded coming out of Dad's mouth instead of Ima's.

"Okay," Ima said. She didn't sound happy, but neither was she particularly upset.

A teeny-tiny ball of hope sparked up inside Lara. Maybe all of this . . . stuff . . . wasn't the end of the world. Maybe everything really would work out, just like Dad said. Maybe . . .

"You don't believe me." Dad's words cut through the wooden door and Lara cringed on reflex.

"We do not need to have this conversation right now. We're not accomplishing anything." Ima's neutral tone had disappeared.

"Just like I'm not accomplishing anything, right? I'm the useless one. Again."

It was undeniable. Dad had started to yell. At the harsh sound Lara's fingers immediately embarked on a frantic dance outside of her control. She could hear Caroline whimper next to her. As the older sister, she probably ought to lead Caroline back to the safety of their bedroom. But she absolutely could not stand the thought of being cooped up in there, knowing that just two doors down Dad and Ima were . . .

No. It was better to stay here. At least then she'd know for sure what was going on. Even if that knowledge hardly brought comfort.

Ima's clipped words snapped Lara's attention away from her sister. "There is no need to read so much into everything. I did not say any of those terrible things."

"You don't need to say it," Dad said. "I can feel it in the way you look at me. How you always ask me about how looking for a job is going, as though you're expecting me to fail."

Barely contained tears punctuated his voice, jolting Lara to her very core. She didn't recall seeing her father really cry. Ever. Even at Grandpa's funeral, he'd only gotten a bit watery around the eyes.

Then Ima spoke again, and her anger was so thick, Lara could practically feel it. "But I didn't say it. This is just you blaming me for your insecurities. Again."

Lara gulped.

Muffled words came through the door, but Lara could no longer devote her full attention to deciphering them. Instead she observed, with no small amount of horror, the unwelcome sight of Benny bouncing down the hallway. He went straight for the observation spot Lara and Caroline had so carefully staked out.

Lara silently willed her brother to be quiet and just pass them by. But she might as well have wished for a snowstorm in Seattle in the middle of August. It just was not going to happen.

"Hey guys!" Benny said. Goodness, did he really have to talk quite so loudly all the time? "Whatchya doing?"

"Nothing." Lara didn't dare speak too loudly. Still, Benny needed to understand that he absolutely could not just come over here and talk at a typical Benny volume right now. "Go away."

Lara thought her words sounded properly stern, but it might not be enough. Benny had an odd kind of immunity to sternness, especially when it came from her.

"It doesn't look like you're doing nothing!" If anything, Benny's voice had gotten several notches louder. "It looks like you're spying. On Dad and Ima! Wow! Are you guys spying?"

"Of course not," Lara replied, but even she knew there was little to no conviction in her voice. "We're just . . ."

She trailed off as she tried and failed to come up with a remotely decent excuse.

"Just spying! Spying!" Benny repeated.

Lara didn't bother denying it.

With a few crashing footsteps, Benny jammed himself in between the two sisters. Lara couldn't quite believe that Dad and Ima hadn't already come out to check on the commotion and give all of them a talking-to.

She leaned back against the door, not bothering to keep quiet. There wasn't any point to it.

Usually, Benny had a unique talent for only paying attention to the things he wanted to bother with while blissfully ignoring everything else. He was sort of like Dad in that way. Still, Lara knew the very instant he finally started tuning in to what was going on inside the bedroom. She would have known it even if he hadn't blurted out a word that he most definitely was not supposed to say. Ever.

"Shut up," Lara told him.

Ima had somehow managed to ignore Lara and Caroline investigating—okay, spying—by the door and Benny trampling into the situation. Yet she would not—perhaps could not—ignore the sound of Benny exclaiming a Very Bad Word.

The door swung open, revealing Ima's fierce scowl. Her dark hair had fallen out of its usual neat bun, and red circles rimmed her eyes.

Lara stared. Ima wasn't supposed to cry. It was one of the basic rules of the universe. Then again, Dad and Ima also weren't supposed to yell at each other.

"Benjamin, please do not use that word in my presence again. Or out of my presence, for that matter." Then she turned to Lara. "And you, Lara Ezter! Perhaps you might explain what exactly you're doing outside of my bedroom?"

Georgia Ketteridge always had an excuse ready when she got caught eavesdropping on important conversations. But Lara Finkel's brain went completely blank as her mother's eyes bored into her.

"I was . . . we were . . . I mean . . ." she attempted.

"They were spying on you!" Benny said. When Lara glared at him, he shrugged. "What? I was just telling the truth."

Lara almost snorted. If everyone told the truth, there'd be no need for spying in the first place. Clearly, things had changed around here. And not for the better.

Ima only sighed. "I suppose you heard our discussion, then."

"Yes," Lara said. "We did."

Although she was bursting with questions, she couldn't bring herself to say anything more.

"Well. I am very sorry you had to hear that," Ima said. "You shouldn't have. Now. Everyone, please return to your bedrooms for some quiet time before dinner."

Lara did not dare to contradict her mother.

CHAPTER FIFTEEN:

UNSWEET DREAMS

LOCATION: House, 7:00 p.m. (approximately)

EVENT: Dad and Ima had a really bad fight.

QUESTION FOR FURTHER INVESTIGATION: Why do people who love each other hurt each other so much?

For Lara, going to sleep wasn't an easy task at the best of times. And this most certainly wasn't the best of times.

She rolled over and glanced at the glowing red lights of her alarm clock. It was 2:43. She sighed. That left her with hardly any time at all before she'd have to wake up and drag herself to school.

Dark as it was, she couldn't see her sister. But Lara guessed that Caroline was still awake in her own bed. She just had a feeling.

"Lina-Lin?" Lara said in a loud-ish whisper. Caroline was a notoriously heavy sleeper, so it shouldn't disturb her if she really had managed to fall asleep.

A grunt came from the next bed. Lara had been right.

Soon, Caroline's computer voice spoke. Caroline had turned the volume down on her tablet, but the room was quiet enough that Lara had no problem making out the words.

"Are Dad and Ima going to be okay?" Caroline asked.

Lara winced. Her sister certainly hadn't wasted time on trivial matters. Generally, Lara appreciated this, but after today's events she wouldn't have minded a little useless chatter.

"Of course!" she told her sister. She hoped very much that she sounded sufficiently confident. Caroline had enough to worry about without throwing their parents' marriage into the mix.

"How can you be sure?"

In truth, Lara was not sure at all. But she couldn't share that with her sister. Her mind raced to find a lie that sounded at least a little bit true.

"Because it's just one fight," she said finally. It was the best she could do. "People don't . . . you know . . . because of just one fight."

Lara did not mention the fact that Dad and Ima rarely fought at all. Or that this particular fight was way scarier than any other fight she could recall. Caroline probably knew that already.

"I guess you're right," Caroline responded after a pause. As usual, her computer voice gave nothing away about her state of mind.

"We should try to go to sleep," Lara said. She had no desire to discuss the subject further. Hopefully, Caroline would get the hint.

Caroline didn't answer. But about ten minutes later snores came from her side of the room.

More glowing numbers changed on the clock, and still Lara could not find sleep. Finally, she decided to get out of bed. Lying there clearly wasn't accomplishing anything. If she had to be up, she could at least enjoy a glass of milk.

Lara tiptoed out of her room. She didn't think anyone else was up—how could they be?—but she didn't want to risk causing a disturbance. Once she reached the bottom of the stairs, she slipped toward the kitchen. But when she reached the door outside of the den, Lara paused. A sliver of light poked out from underneath the door. As she drew closer, Lara heard laughter.

She opened the door to find her mother, sitting on the couch watching an old-timey show on TV. The volume was on low, but she could still hear the fake laughter punctuating every line.

Ima turned toward her. "What are you doing here, Lara-bear?"

"I couldn't sleep." Lara tried to sound casual. As though finding her mother watching sitcoms in the middle of the night was a regular occurrence.

With a weary sigh, Ima beckoned Lara toward the couch. "I suppose I have an idea of why that might be."

Lara plopped down on the middle cushion and curled herself into a human-sized ball. Despite the many thoughts and fears gnawing at her mind, she could not think of a single thing to say. So she just said "Yeah."

"I apologize for not telling you sooner about your father's . . . situation," Ima continued. "I wanted to tell all of you from the very beginning, but he . . . well, never mind that. You know now, and I want to reassure you that we'll be okay. I make enough money for us to get by."

Nodding, Lara did not bother to inform her mother that she'd known about Dad's "situation" long before this afternoon. "Okay," she said, her voice rather smaller than usual.

"Okay," her mother repeated. "We are going to be okay. We've gotten through hard things before as a family and we can do it again."

Lara didn't say anything more. She wasn't sure what words could do right now.

She should probably go back to bed. But she didn't want to. Instead, Lara started rocking herself. Back and forth, back and forth again. Her movements matched the strokes of Ima's hands across her back.

Somehow, it all made her feel just a little bit better.

Eventually, Ima pulled Lara forward and planted a soft kiss on the top of her head. "I think it is time for you to go back to sleep."

And so Lara retreated to her room. Yet it would be quite a while until sleep arrived.

CHAPTER SIXTEEN:

IN WHICH THE INVESTIGATION RESUMES

Lara had never officially closed the Case of the Gross Brisket. And one question kept nagging at her: Why *did* Dad lose his job? After her parents' fight, she absolutely had to know. Obviously, she needed to continue the case. If she could just figure that out, then maybe everything would be okay again.

First, she needed to review her notes. Lara pulled out her detective notebook and went back to the very beginning. Caroline glanced at her from the other side of the room, but Lara ignored it. She needed to focus.

"Are you still doing fiasco business?" Caroline asked.

She had spelled out the word rather than the acronym when typing out her question. Quite generously, Lara ignored the mistake.

"Maybe," she said.

"I don't think that's a good idea. We shouldn't get involved in Dad and Ima's business. Besides, what else is there to investigate?" Caroline asked. "We figured out why Dad is upset."

Lara scowled. Georgia Ketteridge would never drop a case if there was still a huge question hanging out there. She would try to figure everything out.

"I decide when FIASCCO's cases are closed. It's still open if I say it is. And I say that I want to find out why Dad lost his job." Lara said her words firmly. After a moment, she added, "Besides, I don't know any other mysteries that need solving."

"What about Ima's brooch? It's been missing for a week now. Don't you think that should be investigated?"

Huh? What brooch? Then, Lara remembered. Ima had lost her special brooch and was asking everyone to keep an eye out for it. Lara resisted the urge to roll her eyes. That was hardly the kind of case worthy of FIASCCO.

"She probably just left it in a box somewhere. Or loaned it to Aunt Miriam or something."

"Maybe. Maybe not. Why don't you try to find out?"

Lara sighed through gritted teeth. "Because it's a really boring mystery! I told you, I'm going to take care of things with Dad. If you're so interested in Ima's brooch, you find it."

"Maybe I will," Caroline said. But she did not seem very enthusiastic about the idea.

Lara straightened her back and picked up her pen again. No matter what Caroline thought, she was going to figure this out. She considered the options. Maybe she could find top secret information on his computer? Hacking into other people's computers was one of Georgia's favorite tactics.

The problem was, Lara had no hacking skills whatsoever. Well, okay. Lara wouldn't need to hack anything. She could just sneak into Dad's office and borrow his laptop for a bit.

That led to another problem: How could Lara get into Dad's office without him noticing?

She considered sneaking in under cover of night, then dismissed the idea as too risky. Her parents' bedroom was right next to Dad's office, and Ima was a notoriously light sleeper. Lara did not relish the idea of having to explain what she was doing in the office at midnight. So, she'd have to sneak in during the daytime. She just needed the right distraction. Fortunately, she could recruit an accomplice.

Lara barged into Benny and Noah's room. She kept her eyes alert to avoid tripping on the many thingamabobs spread out over Benny's half of the floor. Lara had long since stopped bothering to track exactly what objects

Benny had claimed for his projects. So long as he wasn't trying to use any of her things, she didn't care.

And there was Benny, tinkering with paper clips on his bed.

"If you're here to help me with my machine, then you can't," Benny informed her. "The contest rules say that only the inventor can build it."

"I am not here to help with your machine." Lara, diplomatic as always, did not point out her lack of interest in such a thing. "I have something else for you to do."

Benny didn't look up from his contraption. "Why should I? You're not the boss of me."

Fortunately, Lara had anticipated this very response. "Because if you do me a tiny little favor, I'll give you two of my hairclips for . . . for whatever you're doing."

"Deal," he said instantly, bouncing off the bed with a flourish.

Lara fidgeted with the edge of her shirt. "I'm so glad we could come to an agreement. So, here's the plan. I need you to create a distraction downstairs while I . . . do something important."

There was no need to tell Benny exactly what she planned to do. That would just invite more questions.

Her brother's grin appeared positively devilish. "If

you'd told me that's what it was, I would have done it for free."

"I'll keep that in mind. So do you have any ideas?"

"Yeah! Maybe a smoke grenade! I was reading on the Internet about how to make one, and—"

"No! No explosions or smoke or anything else that puts the house at risk of total destruction."

For goodness' sake, Lara added silently. Maybe Lara wasn't exactly being the most responsible big sister at the moment, but she could at least set a few common-sense rules.

"But you said you wanted a distraction."

"And I do. Just something a little less dangerous. Please. Come on," Lara prodded. "You have to have some ideas."

After Lara vetoed a few of Benny's more outrageous suggestions, the plan was finalized. Lara headed for the hallway bathroom—her designated waiting spot for the mission. As she squatted by the sink, she tried to ignore the ache in her knees and the heartbeat hammering through her chest.

Right on cue, a loud crash sounded from downstairs. Benny's loudest voice followed a moment later. "Daaad!" he cried. The panic in his voice sounded very real even to Lara.

"Coming," Dad said. Heavy footsteps thumped down the hall, past Lara's hiding spot.

Lara slipped out of the bathroom. Dad was nowhere to be found, and he'd left the office door wide open.

Before she could talk herself out of it, Lara made straight for the laptop. Guessing his password was easy—nlcb777. Really, using the first initials of Lara and her siblings was quite uncreative.

Unfortunately, Dad's desktop was a mess, with approximately a jillion icons crammed together. There was little order to any of it. A recipe for apple turnovers. The handbook for Pinecone Arts Academy parents. A whole lot of files with useless names like "doc3."

"Come on," Lara whispered. Surely there had to be something relevant in all of this.

Ah. There it was, right next to Spider Solitaire: a file called "termination letter."

Lara emailed the document to herself quickly, then raced out of the office. Mission complete.

She let herself into Benny and Noah's bedroom. She'd promised Benny hair clips in exchange for his help, and she intended to deliver. The clips sat in her pocket—a necessary sacrifice for Benny's assistance.

The loud voices coming from downstairs told Lara that Benny's distraction had not yet ended.

Lara sat on Noah's desk chair and examined the room. Her older brother's half of it was not particularly neat, but neither was it messy. A pennant for his high school was mounted on the wall surrounded by pictures of Noah and his friends. His physics textbook sat open on the desk, right next to a manual on auto repairs. Lara frowned. How horrifically dull! She couldn't imagine why her brother would want to actually read that thing. Well, that wasn't her concern.

Next, she considered Benny's part of the room. Now that really was a total disaster. Lara marveled that he was even able to make it to his bed, what with the sprawling morass of his latest invention taking up most of the floor. She remembered him saying that it was a Rube Goldberg machine. Which apparently meant going to a whole lot of trouble to do something really easy like zipping a zipper. It all seemed kind of pointless, though she knew better than to say so.

Lara surveyed the hodgepodge of materials he'd gathered: a month's worth of empty cereal boxes, shiny black marbles, several rolls of twine. He'd also borrowed—or just taken—buttons from Aunt Miriam's sewing kit, Caroline's empty acrylic tubes, and . . . wait. What was that silver oval on the far side of the floor?

She moved closer and her mouth dropped. Although the turquoise engravings had become blackened and gunky, she felt reasonably certain that this was Ima's missing brooch. Somehow, Benny had found it. Now he was using it as part of his weird machine thing.

"You're not supposed to see the machine until it's done."

Lara jumped at the sound of Benny's voice. She'd been so distracted by this newest revelation that she hadn't noticed him come in.

Her brother looked perfectly oblivious as always. Maybe he didn't even realize that he was using Ima's treasured heirloom like it was just another piece of junk. She should probably tell him. Or Ima.

Later, she decided. Right now there were other priorities. She smiled at him and handed over the hair clips. "Thanks for the help."

"No problemo. If you ever need me to crash my car around again, tell me!"

It was silly, perhaps, but Lara didn't fully release her

breath until she returned to her room. Caroline wasn't there. Good. If the stuff about Dad was really bad, then she wouldn't have to tell her sister.

As her foot tapped out a nervous dance, Lara pulled up her email. Clicked on the message she'd sent from Dad's computer. And started to read.

"Dear Mr. Finkel . . ." the letter began. Blah blah blah. That wasn't important.

Then, about halfway down the page, she found it. A section called "reason for termination." Lara read.

"Despite the high quality of your work, your consistent inability to meet deadlines and complete administrative tasks have caused problems . . ."

Lara stared. She couldn't say she was surprised. Paperwork and deadlines definitely weren't Dad-things. It all made sense now—Ima's irritation, Dad's embarrassment, all the secret-keeping. Even so, Lara couldn't help but feel as though she'd been kicked.

She had solved the mystery. But she had absolutely no idea how she—or anyone else—could fix it.

CHAPTER SEVENTEEN:

A CRIME MOST BLOODY

Caroline wanted the rest of the world to go away forever. Unfortunately, the world wasn't inclined to go away just because she wished it so. And she did not quite have the energy to yell at Lara for her continued meddling into everyone else's business, no matter how much the idea appealed to her.

As the next-best option, Caroline threw herself into research. She had promised Micah that she would help figure out how to get back at Marissa and she intended to do just that. If her stomach still clenched a bit at the thought, well, that was easy enough to ignore.

After all, she told herself, she and Micah were just going to do a harmless prank. It wasn't as if they were going to do something really mean. Like calling Marissa useless.

Caroline gulped. She did not want to think about Dad and Ima, she did not.

Legs bouncing, Caroline stared intently at her phone. Like always, she was texting with Micah. However, their current topic of conversation was not one of Caroline's favorites.

So, what should we do to Marissa? We have to get back at her.

Although Caroline had hoped that Micah would eventually drop his plan for revenge, he had not. It definitely didn't help that Marissa had loudly referred to them as "losers" in the cafeteria today. When Micah snapped back at her, she'd shrugged and said that she didn't realize Caroline understood the word *loser*. At which point Caroline barely managed to restrain her friend from punching Marissa in the face.

So she was pretty sure there was no talking Micah out of anything. Caroline bounce-walked over to her computer and entered "pranks for school" into Google. Maybe it was better if she, not Micah, decided on the prank. Surely she could find something that wasn't too mean. They'd still give Marissa a small fright, of course, but they wouldn't do any lasting damage in the process.

After watching three different videos on YouTube, Caroline had an idea. She reached for the phone again.

Let's mess with her pens. Like take a black pen and make it purple.

*I found out how to do it on
YouTube.*

Micah wrote back almost immediately.

Cool idea.

Caroline beamed. She'd done it. Micah liked her idea, he was still her friend, and they weren't going to do anything too mean to Marissa. Caroline thought she'd like it if someone made a boring black pen turn purple. Marissa probably wouldn't, but even she couldn't possibly get particularly angry at such a minor nuisance. Right?

Still, Caroline couldn't entirely shake the lump that had taken up residence in her chest—the one that had nothing to do with Micah or Marissa or any of this. No, this particular lump had formed while she stood outside her parents' bedroom, listening as everything fell apart in the worst way possible.

It was a blank-canvas-brain moment if ever there was one.

Don't think about it, Caroline!

Her favorite therapist always said that whenever things got to be too much, she ought to find something relaxing to do. Something that would make her forget about her worries, if only for a brief moment. But what?

A ping from her phone tore Caroline away from her spiraling thoughts. Micah, it seemed, had a lot to say about the plan to avenge Helena the zebra. Okay, so not exactly the distraction she'd been looking for, but still a distraction.

I like it.

But I think I can make it even better.

Three dots popped up on the screen, signaling that Micah was still typing something. Caroline had begun to think of them as the dreaded dots of uncertainty. She leaped up from her desk chair. While she waited for the rest of Micah's plan, she paced. Caroline counted six steps when a new message popped up.

Do you think Marissa is afraid
of blood?

She frowned deeply. Although she'd started to get used to Micah's more unusual ideas, she couldn't begin to guess how blood connected to her pen-color-switching scheme. She quickly tapped out a response:

??

Truly, Caroline could have typed more than two question marks. She certainly had more than two questions. Did Micah's plan involve hurting Marissa? How did he plan to do such a thing without getting caught? And, most importantly, was it at all possible to talk him out of it now? Or at least to back out of it?

A stream of new messages appeared soon enough.

Don't worry

It's not real blood

I saw some videos about pranks that use pens

One of them showed how to make a pen drip fake blood

Like the stuff for Halloween

My dad's taking me to the Halloween store this weekend

Marissa's going to get it all over her drawings

Bet she doesn't know the difference between real blood and fake

Caroline allowed herself a tiny sigh. Knowing that they were not, in fact, scheming to physically injure Marissa came as a relief. Still, was it really fair to sabotage Marissa's artwork like that?

Sure it is, came a voice from Caroline's head. *It's exactly what she did to you.*

Even so, Caroline's hands shook a bit as she wrote out her response to Micah.

Okay.

She already knew she wasn't going to sleep well tonight.

***

LOCATION: Breakfast table, 7:00 a.m.

EVENT: C. checked her phone a bajillion times (approximately speaking). Did not respond when I very nicely asked her to pass the milk.

QUESTION FOR FURTHER INVESTIGATION: Why is my sister keeping secrets from me?

Lara had so wanted a distraction from her discoveries about Dad. For better or worse, she now had one. Caroline was most definitely up to something. The first clue was the way Caroline kept checking her phone over breakfast. Not that this was unusual. Ever since school had started, Caroline's phone had practically been glued to her hand. Normally, she wore a bright grin as she tapped away at it, talking to this mysterious friend of hers. Today she still stared at the screen, but her responses were brief. The corner of her mouth twitched every time the phone pinged.

Very suspicious indeed.

The second clue was the way Caroline reacted to Dad and Ima—or rather, her total lack of reaction. Barely a dozen words passed between the parents throughout the entire morning, and six of them were Ima's very cool announcement: "I'll take the kids to school."

Dad nodded. He didn't even bother glancing up from his phone.

By instinct, Lara glanced over to Caroline so that they could have one of their wordless conversations. But she too kept her eyes fixed on her phone, seemingly unaware of everything else.

It all just irritated Lara. Was she the only one who cared about Dad and Ima and the catastrophe that was unfolding between them? What could possibly be so important to Caroline that she would just ignore the rest of them in favor of her phone?

She didn't like it even a little bit.

When Ima finally dropped them off at school, Caroline didn't bother saying goodbye to any of them before heading off who knows where. It was then that Lara made a decision. She was going to follow Caroline and figure out what, exactly, had so captured her sister's attention.

Today, Lara's first class was orchestra. The teacher didn't seem to notice Lara much, thanks to her complete lack of musical talent. So she probably wouldn't notice Lara slipping in late. That left plenty of time for her mission.

The real trick, she knew, would be to observe Caroline without Caroline observing her. Lara tried to imagine what Georgia Ketteridge would do, but the books were sadly lacking in detailed instructions on how to spy on your sister.

She did her very best to look normal as she walked over to the main sixth-grade hallway. It teemed with kids laughing, talking, and in one case, practicing an energetic dance routine. On the plus side, all the people made it easy to avoid being spotted by Caroline. On the minus side, the people made it difficult to actually see Caroline.

Lara took in a deep breath as she wove through the masses. She narrowly avoided being kicked in the chest by a dancer who clearly had no manners. Lara clenched her jaw and scanned the sea of people. Where was Caroline?

Ah! There she was—standing at the corner of a corridor talking to a boy with thick glasses and an X-Men T-shirt. So this must be her new friend.

Lara narrowed her eyes at him. They were talking about something—or rather, the boy was talking excitedly, hands flying about. Maybe it wasn't fair, but Lara couldn't help but feel suspicious of the mysterious boy who had started sucking up all of her sister's time and attention.

She had to get closer to them.

It was risky, she knew, but Lara pushed through more people. Soon, Caroline and her friend were only five feet away, then four. Caroline's back faced Lara, so Caroline did not notice anything amiss. Probably.

Lara leaned up against a locker and tried her best to look like she wasn't eavesdropping.

". . . so I got a whole bunch of fake blood," the boy was saying. "This is gonna be great."

Lara's first instinct was to shudder at the mention of blood—even fake blood. Her second was to frown. What did her sister need with fake blood? It was almost two months until Halloween! Exactly what kind of an influence did this boy have on Caroline?

She could not make out Caroline's response. Annoying! Luckily, the boy had a habit of talking at a rather loud volume. Lara didn't know how her sister could possibly stand it.

"We'll do it during class today!" he said.

Do what?

Lara frowned. There was something going on here.

Maybe Caroline refused to talk to her sister about it—for some completely nonsensical reason—but Lara would figure it out herself.

Suddenly, the warning bell shrieked. Lara covered her ears with her hands. By the time the awful noise stopped, Caroline and the boy were gone.

She wanted to know more. But try as she might, she could not think of any practical way to spy on her sister during class.

Lara sighed and scurried back to the seventh-grade hallway. At least she'd learned one thing: Caroline and her new friend were doing something very odd. Something that involved fake blood.

She scribbled in her notebook:

PROBLEM: C. is up to something with a v. suspicious boy. He likes fake blood (seriously eww).

It appeared as though FIASCCO's work was far from complete.

CHAPTER EIGHTEEN:

THE DISTRACTION

Caroline found it pretty much impossible to concentrate on anything during her first few classes of the day. Even getting to second-period language arts proved to be a difficult task. After numerous wrong turns, Caroline just barely slipped into the classroom on time. Actually paying attention in class was not going to happen. The whole time, she felt squiggly spirals of paint swirling around in her mind—yellows and oranges, mostly, with a few streaks of red. Bloodred, of course.

Finally, the moment arrived. Experimental Art class with Micah—and Marissa.

Micah was already waiting for her at their usual table. He winked at her and Caroline gulped in about a gallon of air.

Logically, Caroline knew that their plan was still top secret. Even so, she felt certain that anyone who happened to look could see "PLANNING TO DO A VERY BAD THING" painted across her forehead. In fancy red script.

Marissa was sitting on the far side of the room, sur-

rounded by a group of admirers as she lined up her colored pens.

"We have to wait for the right moment," Micah told
Caroline in a whisper. "Not right away."

Caroline nodded. It made sense. At the same time, she
couldn't help but hope that the right moment—whatever
that was—wouldn't arrive today. Or any other day, for that
matter.

Soon enough, Caroline was sculpting away at her
giraffe. At least, she attempted to sculpt. She nearly cut
the poor thing's left ear off before giving up.

"Are you ready?" Micah asked her. He didn't even pretend to work on the charcoal drawing in front of him.

Caroline didn't want to say yes. But she didn't want to
say no, either. Instead she gave her friend a small, tight
smile and hoped that would be enough.

Sometimes, not talking with mouth-words had its
perks.

"Cool," he said. "I'll be the one doing the . . . you know.
You can be the distraction. When I say it's time, you'll
start the distraction. I'll take care of everything else."

Caroline stared into the nostrils of her clay giraffe and
wished fervently for a fire drill.

They'd talked about all of this before, of course. Caroline had even come up with a plan for how to cause a distraction. Except with the big moment looming ahead, she could not remember any of it.

She had to tell Micah that she just wasn't ready. Yet when she glanced over at him and saw the beginnings of a bursting grin . . . well, she didn't want to be the one to talk the smile off his face.

How hard could it be to make a distraction, really? She could make something up when the time came.

"It's time," Micah whispered at last.

Caroline tore her eyes away from the giraffe, which had started to take on a rather sad expression. Before she could think too much about it, she marched to the other end of the room where slabs of clay were kept. Closer to Marissa.

Even though she didn't need more clay, Caroline cut herself a nice big piece of it. The feeling of the cool, wet clay in her hands soothed her.

Okay. Now she needed to distract.

Instead of returning to her own workstation, Caroline wandered over to Marissa's table. She managed to get close enough to see Marissa's drawing. It was a rather nice drawing, full of brightly colored flowers. Whatever else one might say about Marissa (and Caroline had plenty of not-nice things to say), she was not without artistic skill.

"Hello? Are you lost?"

Caroline snapped to attention.

Without her tablet, she could only shake her head.

"Sorry? I don't think I understood you. You might want to try actually talking."

"That's not very nice!" another girl scolded. "She can't help it that she's . . . you know."

Caroline clenched her teeth. She did not know exactly what her supposed defender meant to call her, but she knew she didn't like it. "You know" indeed!

Face-to-face with Marissa's awfulness once more, Caroline didn't feel at all bad about what she and Micah had planned. Well, not too bad, at least.

Still clutching her slab of clay, Caroline moved closer to Marissa. She didn't have a destination, she didn't have a plan. She just knew that she wanted to wipe that annoying smirk off Marissa's face.

Caroline tripped. The clay flew away from her hands and headed straight toward Marissa.

The other girls shrieked. Caroline covered her ears at the sound. She really, really hadn't meant for this to happen.

And yet it had been the perfect distraction.

Marissa had managed to dodge out of the way before being hit with a clay projectile. The girl next to her—the one who had tried to defend Caroline—was not so fortunate. Wet clay now clung to the front of her frilly white shirt. She gave Caroline a glare so vicious that Caroline would have gladly turned to clay herself.

Without her tablet, Caroline couldn't really say sorry. She hoped that this girl would know that she really did feel sorry.

Chaos descended on the art room as Ms. Williamson rushed forward to offer the girl several trees' worth of paper towels.

"It's no use! I can't walk around in this shirt for the rest of the day." She stared at Caroline. "Why'd she spill this all over me anyway? She's not even supposed to be here."

Caroline felt her skin prickle. It was, of course, true that she wasn't supposed to be around the table. She certainly did not want to be there. But it sounded to her like this girl was saying something else.

She's not even supposed to be here. Here, as in the table? Or here, as in Pinecone Arts Academy? Caroline tapped her hands against the edge of her shirt.

"Now," Ms. Williamson said in a voice Caroline recognized as strained. "It was just an accident. I'm sure Caroline is very sorry. Aren't you?"

Cheeks blushing furiously, Caroline nodded. In the periphery of her vision, she could see a familiar shape messing around with pens. So Micah had been able to take advantage of the distraction.

Having at least attempted an apology, Caroline raced back to the relative safety of her own table. Her giraffe's sad face greeted her. A few minutes later, Micah slid into the seat next to hers.

"Good job with the distraction," he said.

Caroline did not feel like she had done a good job at anything.

She made a half-hearted attempt to add more definition to her giraffe's spots and tried very hard not to look at Marissa's table. After just a few strokes of her carver, yet another scream came from the other side of the room.

"Goodness," Ms. Williamson said as she hurried over to Marissa's table. "Is there a problem? Again?"

Maybe Caroline was just imagining it, but she thought their teacher sounded more tired than usual.

"Yes, there is a problem!" Marissa said. Caroline winced at the volume.

Marissa held up her drawing. Even from the other side

of the room, Caroline could make out the red splotches mixed in among the intricately drawn flowers. Caroline flapped her hands.

She deserves it, Caroline reminded herself. Besides, it was just fake blood—even if it looked awfully real.

Next to her, Micah stood completely still. But Caroline could make out the beginnings of a smile tugging at his lips.

"Good job, Finkel," he whispered to her. "We did it!"

Caroline did her best to smile back, but succeeded only in a twisted grimace.

The color her brain painted was a dark, dreary gray.

CHAPTER NINETEEN:

THE INTERROGATION

For the next several class periods, Caroline tiptoed through Pinecone Arts Academy filled with the certain dread that she was about to be caught. Every time she entered a new classroom, her heart pounded. She was positive that Principal Jenkins was going to walk in at any moment to drag her into the office. Caroline could practically see the frown on the principal's face as she delivered a lecture about how very disappointed she was. "After all this trouble we've gone to to accommodate you," Principal Jenkins said in her mind. "You've done something terrible to one of your normal classmates. I'm sorry, Caroline Finkel, but we're going to have to ask you to leave this school."

But as the hours ticked by and no one showed up to take her away, she slowly began to relax. Maybe she'd gotten away with it.

The thought did not fill Caroline with joy, and anxious lime-green dots continued to dance through her brain.

Dad picked them up on time once school came to an

end, much to Caroline's relief. But even after such a terrible day, Caroline noticed something odd about Lara. Something that didn't seem quite right.

"How was your day?" Lara asked, with more intensity than seemed warranted.

Caroline pressed a button on her speech app and closed her eyes. "Fine."

"Oh?" Lara asked.

Sighing, Caroline pressed the same button again. "Fine."

Surely Lara would get the message that Caroline was not in a talking mood. Unfortunately for Caroline, her sister did not care.

"I'm just asking because today seems like a rather interesting day. Some might say it's a bloody interesting day."

Bloody? Surely Lara couldn't be implying anything. After all, how could she possibly know what had happened? True, Marissa had been complaining about the injustice of it all day. But Caroline was pretty sure her sister didn't know Marissa. She felt even surer that her sister did not care about Marissa's art.

So why was she throwing around that word?

Maybe Lara was just trying to talk like a British person,

Caroline reasoned. She knew that British people said "bloody" when they wanted to sound particularly cool. Back when Caroline changed to a new computer voice, she'd learned all about British-isms. True, Lara hadn't ever spoken in British-isms before, but maybe she was starting some kind of new experiment? After all, Georgia Ketteridge had a British mom.

Caroline would just have to ignore her sister. She swiped away from her speech app and tapped her fingers against the tablet cover. That should tell Lara how very much she did not want to talk right now.

Lara, however, kept at it. "It was a bloody interesting day," she repeated. "Don't you just love the word *bloody*? Bloody bloody bloody."

The skin on Caroline's neck prickled. Something was off about the whole thing. Lara was fond of many words, but *bloody* generally was not among them. It probably had something to do with her general squeamishness.

She had to play it cool. Caroline opened her speech app once more. "Stop saying 'bloody.' You know I'm the British one in the family," she typed. Her computer voice sounded especially clipped and British-y, much to Caroline's satisfaction.

A sly smile crept onto Lara's face. "That you are," she said. "Speaking of which. I bet you're making all kinds of friends at school, aren't you?"

Caroline frowned. She did not see any discernible connection between her alleged Britishness and her school friends. Probably because there wasn't any. Lara was up to something.

"I have friends," Caroline said. She saw no need to elaborate on the subject any further.

"Mmm-hmm. You looked awfully—I mean. I know you're friends with a boy in your grade."

Staring at the interface of the tablet, Caroline dearly wished that the software program could somehow make up words for her. Too bad she'd just have to rely on her own intuition.

"Go away, Lara," she typed.

A dark eyebrow jerked upward. "My goodness! Someone seems to be in a bad mood today. I wonder why?"

Somehow, Caroline felt as though anything she might say would just incriminate her further. Which was ridiculous, of course, since Lara wasn't really a detective. And she hadn't really committed a crime. Technically, she hadn't even replaced Marissa's pens—that was all Micah.

You were an accomplice, though, her brain helpfully informed her. Caroline knew all about accomplices from the Georgia books.

Enough was enough. Caroline gritted her teeth. With a pointed glare at her sister, she shoved the tablet back into her backpack. Even Lara ought to understand that this conversation was now 100 percent over.

CHAPTER TWENTY:

IN WHICH MAJOR EVIDENCE
IS LOCATED

LOCATION: Home, 6:30 p.m.

EVENT: After highly suspicious activities with an unknown (read: shady) figure this morning, C. is moping around the house. She won't talk to me.

QUESTION FOR FURTHER INVESTIGATION: Why do people change?

Lara rubbed her eyes and stared at her math homework. She'd been working on problem number seven for forever—well, at least for ten minutes—and wasn't any closer to a solution. Her brain kept wandering toward other problems. More interesting and more troublesome problems.

Well, her study skills tutor always said that it was okay to take breaks when she had trouble concentrating. Lara shoved the math problem away and flipped open her detective notebook. The most recent entry—

about Caroline and the highly suspicious boy—stared back at her.

The evidence was, admittedly, rather lacking. But that was no reason why she couldn't speculate about what her sister was up to.

She started to write.

WHAT WERE CAROLINE AND HER FRIEND DOING?—THEORIES

Early Halloween costume planning—possible but kind of boring

Training as a paramedic—no, they're not old enough

Faking somebody's murder—I don't know why they would do that, but it's definitely the most interesting option

Lara tried to invent a scenario in which her sister would be involved in faking a murder. But even she could not imagine such a thing. Caroline was the sort of person who always put away her socks in the right drawer. It was rather difficult to imagine her staging a bloody crime. So far, the Case of the Fake Blood was a total dead end.

Clenching her jaw, Lara flipped through the notebook some more. Caroline's odd behavior wasn't the only mystery she had to solve.

She started a new page.

QUESTION: *Why did Noah take the bus going in the wrong direction last week?*

Lara started to write out a list of possible explanations, but none of them were at all satisfying. She was pretty sure that Noah had not, in fact, started taking trapeze lessons to pursue his secret dream of joining the circus. Still . . . Noah had not yet arrived home, she noted. Was he at the mystery location again?

At the moment, Benny was doing homework in the den. Or, more likely, playing video games while *not* doing his homework. Regardless, Benny and Noah's room was currently unoccupied. And that meant Lara could do some real investigation on the matter of Noah and his secret life.

After double-checking to make sure that Benny was in fact in the den, Lara made her way to her brothers' room.

She wrinkled her nose upon entering. The room stank of dirty socks. Normally Dad and Ima bugged all of them to clean up dirty clothes, but she supposed they'd had other things on their minds as of late.

She hesitated a bit before examining Noah's desk. It was one thing to spy on Caroline, but Noah was the oldest. There was probably some kind of unwritten rule against going through his stuff.

No matter, Lara decided. He was hiding something and she needed to know exactly what it was.

The first few shelves of Noah's desk were full of boring-ness: calculus homework and registration papers for the football team. And that car manual again—very strange.

Lara frowned. Why would Noah have this?

She opened a drawer. At the very top, she found a glossy brochure with "VOCATIONAL SCHOOL: AUTO-MOTIVE MECHANICS" printed in big black letters across the top.

Well. This was most interesting. Noah was supposed to be going to the University of Washington next year. Ima bugged him approximately five times a week about how he needed to get his application in soon.

And Noah always found an excuse to avoid doing it, Lara realized. The last time it happened he had practi-cally snapped at Ima.

She rummaged through his desk for more evidence. Sure enough, she found a purple University of Washing-ton brochure—at the very bottom of Noah's drawer. As if it had been buried.

If Lara was correct—and she felt quite confident that

she was—then her perfect brother had a very big secret. If Ima and Dad knew that he was thinking about not going to college because he wanted to be a car mechanic . . . well, Lara could just hear the commotion that would ensue. In all likelihood, Ima would use some colorful Hebrew vocabulary. The kind of words the Finkel children weren't supposed to repeat.

Loud footsteps interrupted Lara's thoughts. Heart pounding, she spun around. She relaxed when she saw it was only Benny. Him she could handle—even if he was scowling at her rather fiercely.

"Hey! What are you doing in my room?" Benny demanded.

Time to come up with an excuse that sounded at least a little bit true.

"Just looking for a paperweight," she said.

Okay, so maybe that wasn't the greatest excuse ever. A paperweight! *Not your best work, Lara.*

"We don't have any paperweights," Benny pointed out. Lara tried not to grit her teeth.

"Right," she said. "That's why I'm currently leaving. To go find a paperweight . . . um, somewhere else. You know."

Lara made straight for the door. Unfortunately, her brother was still standing there.

Benny crossed his arms around his chest, his scowl intensifying noticeably. "You were spying again. Weren't you?"

"I don't spy on people!"

I investigate them, Lara added silently. Somehow she thought the distinction would be lost on her brother.

"I'm telling everyone!" Benny declared.

That wouldn't do. Lara bit her lip and frantically searched around the messy room, as though it could give her an answer to her current predicament. Her eyes fell on Benny's Rube Goldberg machine. He must have worked on it quite a bit since she'd last visited. Yet as far as she knew, Ima's heirloom was still missing. And that gave Lara an idea.

"If you say that I'm a spy, then I'm going to tell everyone what you've done with Ima's brooch," Lara said. She straightened her back as she talked. Even arched her eyebrow in what she hoped was a menacing expression.

She'd expected her brother to appear terrified. Instead, he just looked confused. "Huh?"

"Ima's brooch!" When that failed to provoke an appropriate response, Lara tried to explain further. "You're using Ima's brooch in your machine. You really don't know that?"

Benny's face twisted in concentration. "Oh! So that's

what the silver-and-green thing is. I was wondering about that."

Sometimes Lara found her brother's cluelessness charming. Now it was just unbelievable. Still, she could definitely use it to her advantage.

"That silver-and-green thing is Ima's family heirloom from Turkey. I'm sure she'd be thrilled to know that you've decided it's best used for zipping a zipper. That is what your weird machine is supposed to do, isn't it?"

He paled. "Please, please don't do that! I'll return it. I swear."

Lara smiled widely. "I won't tell anyone a thing. So long as you don't tell anyone that I was . . . visiting . . . in here."

Benny bounced over to his part of the room. "Okay, okay. I won't tell!"

"We have a deal, then. Excellent."

As Lara left Benny behind, it occurred to her that both of her brothers could be in very big trouble very soon. Well, no matter. That wasn't any of her concern.

CHAPTER TWENTY-ONE:

AN ACT OF DARING

Caroline had thought the Bloody Pen Incident would be the end of this whole nasty Marissa business. It seemed fair enough. Marissa had ruined her sculpture, so she ruined Marissa's drawing. Now that their business was done, Caroline preferred to pretend that Marissa simply did not exist.

Micah had other plans.

She found out all about it during math class. As usual, she sat next to Micah. And as usual, he had a way to entertain them both when things got boring.

They had a system. Whenever Micah had something to say, he'd scribble a note on the edge of his notebook. Caroline had gotten used to his messy handwriting. To respond, she'd type something in her tablet but would not actually press the "speak" button.

It occurred to Caroline that perhaps she should not be using her tablet in such a way during school hours. But she figured that passing notes to a friend was just something normal kids did in middle school. Maybe she had something of an advantage, but that was no reason not to use it.

Caroline rubbed her eyes and stared at her problem set when a cough sounded next to her. She peered over at Micah's notebook. Sure enough, there was a message waiting for her.

We should do something.

She tapped her foot as she tried to come up with a smart response. Sometimes, Micah's suggestions were entirely too vague for her liking.

Like what? she typed finally.

Micah wrote swiftly and confidently:

Another prank on Marissa. The last one was so much fun.

Speaking for herself, Caroline was not sure she could characterize the experience of pranking Marissa as fun. Terrifying, yes. Guilt-inducing, certainly. It was even a little bit exhilarating, once she got past everything else. But fun?

I don't know about that, Caroline typed. *I think Ms. Williamson knows it was you last time.*

It was true. For the past few art classes, Caroline could practically feel the weight of their teacher's eyeballs on them as they worked at their table.

Of course, Micah had a response for that.

So it won't be in art class this time.

Caroline started to type something. She stopped. Deleted her words. Started typing something else—"but won't Marissa start realizing what we're doing?"—when the tap-tapping of shoes against hard floor made her jump a bit.

It was Ms. Garcia, the math teacher. Caroline gulped. Was she about to get into trouble?

"Micah, that doesn't look very much like your problem set," the teacher said.

Part of Caroline had expected Micah to deny it, but he didn't.

"Sorry," he mumbled. "I'll . . . I'll get to work on it."

"Please do," Ms. Garcia said. She wasn't mean, exactly, but even Micah knew he had to listen.

Caroline glanced over at the teacher, waiting to receive a lecture of her own. But it never came.

She frowned. Did Ms. Garcia just not see that she was using her tablet to pass notes to Micah? It was odd—who did she think Micah was talking to, anyway?

Not getting in trouble ought to be a good thing, but Caroline couldn't help but wonder. A rather unpleasant thought gnawed at her. Did Ms. Garcia not realize that she, Caroline Finkel, the girl who talked with a tablet, could break the rules with her friend?

Did it just not occur to her that someone like Caroline could be just as troublesome as anyone else?

It was the same thing with Ms. Williamson, Caroline realized. She obviously realized that Micah had something or other to do with the not-blood splattered all over Marissa's beautiful flowers. But did she realize that Caroline had been his partner in crime?

Lara had suspected something. Caroline knew that much. But even her sister, who ought to know Caroline better than anyone, hadn't gotten close to the truth.

These thoughts troubled Caroline until math class came to a welcome end.

There wasn't much of a chance to talk with Micah as they walked to lunch together. Caroline vowed that one day she would master the trick of using her tablet while she walked, but that day was a long way off. And Micah usually didn't talk about important things when she didn't have the chance to respond—a fact she deeply appreciated about him.

By the time they were eating lunch at their usual table, Caroline had made up her mind. She took in a shaky breath and tapped out her message: "Okay, let's do something to Marissa. But maybe no blood this time."

Caroline bit her lip as she pressed the "speak" button.

She certainly did not want Micah to think that she was uncool. Still, she didn't think she could stomach another blood-related prank. Marissa's scream had been awfully loud.

"Aww. All of the best pranks need blood," he protested. But given the size of his grin, Caroline felt pretty sure that he was just kidding.

"I'm sure you can come up with something," she typed.

"Well, of course I can. I am the prank master, after all. I put blue hair dye in my brother's shampoo over the weekend and it was so epic."

Although Caroline was not sure that epic was the correct word for such a thing, she smiled. "Cool," she typed.

"But how about you, Caro? Your plan with the pens was pretty good. I bet you can come up with something even better this time . . ."

Caroline's mouth quirked upward. Caro. No one else called her Caro. Sometimes Lara or Dad called her Lina-Lin, but that was hardly the same thing. Lina-Lin was a childish name for a child. Caro was someone else entirely. Caro was Micah's friend. Caro was a girl who fought back against her bullies. Caro didn't need help from her big sister.

Caro was cool.

Did Caroline feel like Caro? She wasn't entirely sure. But she could certainly try.

"I can try to find an idea," she tapped.

She didn't feel at all sure of her words, but what else could she say?

"I know you'll come up with something awesome," Micah offered.

Caroline only wished that she shared his confidence.

As she picked at her apple slices and considered the pros and cons of various prank ideas, Caroline's mind turned to Lara. Would Lara prank Marissa? What kind of prank might she do? And—this question gave Caroline particular pause—what would Lara think if she knew?

The other day, Lara had clearly been trying to figure out what Caroline had been up to. Somehow, she'd found out about the fake blood. And, Lara being Lara, she'd turned the whole thing into a mystery to investigate. But she hadn't really found out anything yet. Caroline felt quite sure of that. It probably would never occur to her sister that she was even capable of breaking the rules so badly.

Now Caroline was going to do yet another daring feat. The very idea of it filled her with spiky yellow paint streaks.

Figure this one out, Lara.

CHAPTER TWENTY-TWO:

THE CASE OF THE ANNOYING COUSIN

LOCATION: A.'s room, 3:30 p.m.

EVENT: Sitting waiting for A. to get here so we can do tutoring stuff.

QUESTION FOR FURTHER INVESTIGATION: Can I make it through the next few hours without wanting to send A. on the next plane back to Tel Aviv?

The neatness of Aviva's room really was kind of sickening. She even made her bed with special corners on the sheets! Lara didn't consider herself a slob by Finkel standards, but she certainly saw no need to make her bed beyond tossing a comforter on top of it.

In an effort to avoid messing up the too-perfect room, Lara chose to sit on the floor. Her butt may not be particularly comfortable, but at least she didn't feel like she was somehow ruining Aviva's bizarre need to live in a room that looked like it belonged on one of those TV shows about home decoration.

Lara knew, in a vague sort of way, that she probably shouldn't be in Aviva's room at all. True, they had agreed to meet this afternoon for tutoring. As usual, Lara needed help with math. Aviva certainly wouldn't have been her tutor of choice, but Ima and Dad had not asked Lara's opinion on the matter. So here she was.

Aviva hadn't exactly given permission for Lara to come into the room without her. But since her cousin was more than twenty minutes late—a fact that was most definitely weird—Lara figured it was more or less okay to let herself in. Unfortunately, she now had absolutely nothing to do. And she was sitting in Aviva's room.

Well . . . perhaps there were a few things she could do to pass time. Lara could practically feel the weight of her detective notebook in her bag. By instinct, she began to examine the room. Just with her eyes, of course. Still, she ached to do more.

She absolutely should not be doing this. If Aviva were to do something like this to her, she'd be mad for a week. At least. And yet . . .

Aviva's perfectly neat desk might as well have a flashing light, beckoning Lara toward it.

Lara stepped toward the desk. Stopped. Stared at it.

After all, she reasoned, it's not like Aviva would keep

anything really important in her desk, where anyone could find it. That would just be foolish.

She pulled open the first drawer. It did not surprise Lara to learn that Aviva kept every single piece of homework she'd ever completed. (Which was all of them, of course. Perfect Aviva.) Lara rolled her eyes as she passed through page after page of math homework with "EXCEL-LENT JOB!!" scribbled across the page.

Then, she came across a page that said "SEE ME." Even the words looked scary—red and bright and spiky. Lara started reading the paper. From the looks of it, Aviva had written an essay about her family. Her stomach tied up in knots as she read, "I live with my mother. Last year we moved in with my aunt uncle four cousins. Living with cousins are fun. I do not have brother or sister."

So. Aviva actually liked Lara, or at least she could pretend. That made Lara feel something uncomfortably close to guilt.

But also . . . Aviva was really, really bad at writing in English.

It surprised Lara. Her cousin spoke with an accent, sure, but every word out of her mouth sounded so precise and correct. This essay was anything but.

"SEE ME," Aviva's teacher had written. Hmm. Lara

flipped to the back of the essay. When she saw the grade her cousin had received, she instinctively cringed. That was very, very not good. The teacher had written another note: "If you rewrite this essay, you may receive a higher grade. You can do it!"

Lara frowned at the paper. Did Aviva's teacher mean to be comforting? She herself couldn't imagine being comforted by such a thing. Then again, she'd never received that kind of a grade on a language arts assignment.

The sound of Aviva's voice caused Lara to jump a good inch. Lara slammed the drawer shut, wincing as it banged. She rushed over to her spot on the floor and did her very best to appear as though she hadn't just invaded her cousin's things.

"Hi," Lara managed to say.

"Oh!" Aviva's mouth fell into an O-shape. "Hello. I did not know you were here."

"We, uh, talked about it. You're tutoring me in math. Remember?"

"Yes, yes. So sorry you had to wait for me. I hope you were not bored."

If it were possible to disappear into the beige walls of the Finkels' guest room, Lara would have done so. As it was, she could only smile and try to look normal, or at least normal-ish. "I'm never bored," she said. "So, uh. I guess we should get to work?"

Aviva nodded with more-than-usual vigor. "Yes! I know I can help you."

And so for the next fifteen minutes Aviva helped Lara with her geometry homework. She actually was a good tutor. Maybe Lara had a chance of understanding the Pythagorean theorem after all.

Lara tried to ignore the twinge of guilt that had taken up residence in her stomach. At this point, it was not so much a twinge as a bowling ball–sized lump of awfulness. Aviva, as much as she might be annoying, was actually, genuinely nice. Nicer than Lara, for sure. Lara felt pretty sure that spying on a nice person officially made her a terrible person.

Maybe she could try and make it up to Aviva.

"I can help you with language arts if you need it," Lara offered.

Eyes fixed firmly on the floor, Aviva began to flap her hands against her knees. At first, the flaps were slow, but they soon intensified. Lara had to repress the urge to flap herself.

"I don't need help," Aviva said.

"Are you sure?" Lara asked. "You did just help me. A lot. I owe you."

"Okay," her cousin said, her voice rather small. "I guess you can help me with this essay I need to write. About a book we read."

She fidgeted while handing Lara a piece of paper. Lara did her best to look, well, nice.

The essay was a little better than the one Lara had found in the drawer. Still, nearly every sentence had an error. What help could Lara be, really? She had no idea how to explain the difference between *there* and *their*, or when to use a comma.

Chewing her lip, Lara grabbed a pen and started making corrections. Next to her, Aviva continued fidgeting.

"I know it seems like I'm not a good writer. But I am very good at writing in Hebrew," she said.

"I'm sure you are," Lara agreed. "You should see my Hebrew letters. Last year my Hebrew teacher said my alephs looked like the poop emoji."

That hadn't actually been what her teacher said, but it was close enough. Aviva gave a weak smile as Lara mentally congratulated herself. She could be a good cousin. Despite strong evidence to the contrary.

"It is strange how you write backwards in English,"

Aviva said. "Sometimes I do not remember which way to write and I end up writing things backwards."

"Ekil siht?" Lara asked, quirking her eyebrows up.

"What?"

Okay, so maybe this wasn't the best moment for that particular joke.

"I just said 'like this' backwards," she explained.

"Oh."

A long silence filled the air. Lara rushed to fill it. "You know, I find that confusing with Hebrew. It always takes me a while to remember that I'm supposed to read things from left to right, not right to left."

"Actually," Aviva said. "It is the other way around."

Of course Aviva would correct Lara when she was trying to offer some kind of comfort. Lara sighed, but did her best to ignore her irritation. She thought about what her sister would do. Caroline would be nice, no matter what.

"Right," Lara said, waving a hand. "I get left and right mixed up a lot. It drove my ballet teacher up the wall when I took lessons."

"You were a dancer?"

"Sort of? I took lessons. My parents let me stop when I accidentally head-butted another girl during a recital."

Lara had been about seven at the time. Even so, she shuddered at the memory. Aviva gave her a small nod. Her hands had stilled.

"I've never been very good at dancing, either," Aviva said. "I suppose we have some things in common."

"I guess we do." Lara gestured toward the paper. "So, I'll correct your essay and you can make the changes before you turn it in. You need to redo the essay for your language arts teacher, so you must be really busy."

About a nanosecond after the words were out of her mouth, Lara remembered that she wasn't supposed to know about Aviva's language arts essay. Fidgeting with her pen, Lara reflected on the fact that Georgia Ketteridge would never reveal investigation findings to a suspect. Not that Aviva was a suspect, exactly, but it was the same general idea.

"How do you know that I need to redo my language arts essay?" Aviva asked.

Lara's mind raced, searching for a good enough lie. Unfortunately, she could only come up with the most unconvincing thing ever. "I just . . . I just guessed."

For a moment, Aviva didn't respond. She just kind of grunted under her breath. Finally, she spoke once again. "Please do not tell my mother about this."

Lara wasn't sure what she had expected. But it wasn't that. "Okay," she said. "No problem."

"It's not that I want to keep secrets from her," Aviva said. "I just do not want her to worry about me. It is hard for her, being here. I do not want to add to her troubles."

It was difficult for Lara to imagine ever-calm Aunt Miriam being troubled by anything, least of all something related to perfect Aviva. Well, almost-perfect Aviva. But she nodded.

"Your secret is completely safe with me."

CHAPTER TWENTY-THREE:

VERMIN MOST FOUL

It took a lot of time, list-making, and looking up videos on YouTube. But finally, Caroline managed to come up with a perfect prank. Even though it involved blood—well, red paint—it was too perfect not to try.

Micah liked it, too. When Caroline had texted him her plans he'd replied with three thumbs-up emojis, plus a few laugh-crying faces for good measure. He said he just might try it on his brothers soon. Caroline smiled, then got to work making a prop for the prank. That was key if it was going to work at all.

Caroline had done an outstanding job on the art, if she did say so herself. Now they just had to pull the whole thing off without getting caught, murdered, or expelled.

We've done it once, Caroline reminded herself. And no one had suspected a single thing, with the possible exception of Ms. Williamson. And Lara. But Lara, while highly annoying, didn't actually know anything.

The drive to school that morning probably was not

any longer than usual. But it definitely felt longer. As they ran into a red light for approximately the billionth time that morning, Caroline bounced up and down in her seat. She didn't have time for this—she needed to show Micah the results of last night's art project. If you could call it that.

Lara shot Caroline a look, which Caroline proceeded to ignore. There was no way Lara could guess what she had planned, surely.

Finally, Ima pulled the station wagon up by the curb. "Have a good day, girls," she said, glancing at her watch. "And remember to tell all your teachers that you'll be gone for Rosh Hashanah tomorrow."

"Yes, Aunt Ezter," Aviva said, while Lara rolled her eyes.

Caroline ignored them both and went straight for the spot in the sixth-grade hallway where she and Micah met each morning. She'd started to think of it as their spot.

Sure enough, he was waiting for her. "Do you have it?"

She glanced around to make sure they weren't being watched—you could never be too careful when plotting against Marissa. After determining that Marissa did not have spies lurking in the nearest trash can, Caroline pulled open her backpack and showed Micah the project that had consumed her entire evening.

His eyes widened when he took it all in. "It looks so real. How'd you do it?"

Caroline flipped open her tablet to answer. "Kugel has toys that look pretty realistic. But it took a lot of experimenting. I made three of them before I got one that looked right."

"You nailed it," Micah told her. "Caroline Finkel, you are an artist of exceptional ability."

Perhaps Caroline should not have been pleased, but she flushed at the compliment.

"We should be able to complete the plan during art," Caroline said.

"Yep. I think you should have the honors this time."

Sweat practically erupted from Caroline's palms, and she frowned. "Are you sure?"

"Of course, Caro! It was your idea, wasn't it? You should be the one to have all the fun."

Micah might be Caroline's best—only?—friend, but she questioned his ideas about what made for a fun thing to do.

"Okay," she typed.

Maybe pranking Marissa wasn't going to be fun,

exactly. But she was going to do it. Caro did not back down from a good challenge.

The fact that Caroline made it until art class without exploding qualified as a minor miracle. Still, her legs were definitely more jittery than usual as she worked on her sculpture. (Or, well, pretended to work.)

In some ways, this plan was actually easier to pull off than the bloody-pen prank. Thanks to Caroline's careful planning, she wouldn't actually have to get close to Marissa.

She would, however, need to get into Marissa's backpack.

"When are you going to do it?" Micah whispered to her as soon as he slid into the seat next to hers.

After looking around to make sure that no one had overheard, Caroline typed a single word into her tablet: "Soon."

Waiting would just make her lose any shred of bravery she possessed, while causing the bad sort of nerves to skyrocket. Caroline felt quite sure of that. So she had to make her move soon.

Luckily, everyone kept their backpacks at the front of the classroom during class. Ms. Williamson said she didn't want anyone ending up with purple paint splattered on their bags. Caroline personally wouldn't mind a little purple paint to decorate her bag, but today her entire plan depended on this arrangement. Even better: There was a movable cork wall between the bag area and the rest of the classroom.

Obviously, the purpose of the wall was not to hide students who were in the process of doing a not-so-nice thing to a classmate. Caroline knew that, and it made her insides squirm. The artist in the back of her brain kept painting tight spirals in puke green—a fair expression of her mood, to be sure.

Don't be a baby, she scolded herself. It wasn't like Marissa was going to actually get hurt or anything.

Soon after class began, Ms. Williamson disappeared to the far side of the room to help a boy use the wire cutters. It was the perfect opportunity.

Micah knew it too. He smiled at her.

Caroline took in a deep breath and scurried to the bag area.

It wasn't hard at all to find Marissa's backpack. Her name was monogrammed right on it, in white cursive lettering. Caroline's hands shook a little as she unzipped the bag and searched for Marissa's lunch box.

Ah. There it was—one of those fancy lunch boxes with padded fabric. Caroline opened it, careful to avoid touching Marissa's actual food. After all, there was no need to spread germs. (Well, at least not any more than she was already doing.)

Before she could think too much about it, Caroline slipped in her creation. She sealed up the box, zipped the bag, and tiptoed away from it as fast as she could possibly manage—nearly tripping on the way back to her seat.

"Did you do it?" Micah asked her.

Caroline nodded.

Micah gave a laugh that veered toward an honest-to-goodness cackle. Caroline tried to smile back at him.

"This is going to be awesome!" he said. "I can't wait for lunch."

Caroline tried to agree, but couldn't quite manage to figure out the right words. Wild curls in bloodred filled her mind, making it impossible to concentrate. She had absolutely no idea how she was going to make it to lunch.

Yet make it she did—though not without a whole lot of hand-flapping, leg-bouncing, and general lack of ability to pay attention to anything. But finally, she and Micah made it to the cafeteria.

Act normal, Caroline told herself. *And for goodness' sake, don't look at Marissa.*

Of course, she couldn't look away from Marissa.

There wasn't much to look at, not at first. A crowd of girls surrounded Marissa—she, naturally, was at the very center of the group. Soon enough, the cafeteria became so crowded that Caroline couldn't see anything aside from a sea of moving bodies. All the colors and smells swirled together, making it almost impossible to concentrate.

"Are you okay?" Micah asked her.

Caroline did not respond. Nor did she look at her own lunch bag. She just waited.

Soon enough, it came. A familiar shriek rang through the cafeteria. Then, a beat of silence.

It didn't last long. "Someone put a dead rat in my lunch!" Marissa said. Well, screamed.

Murmurs rippled through the room, soon followed by the unmistakable chime of giggling. Caroline smiled, although her conscience winced.

All the chaos made it hard to follow what happened next, but Caroline guessed that a teacher went over to Marissa. "It's not a rat," an unfamiliar voice declared. "Although it does look very realistic."

"Nice job," Micah whispered.

Caroline felt absurdly proud of her handiwork. Because of course she hadn't actually put a dead animal in Marissa's lunch—she would never do something so obviously mean and unsanitary. No, instead she'd merely taken one of Kugel's mouse toys and made it look like it was dead. Large quantities of red paint had been involved.

It was just a joke. Wasn't it?

"You screamed because of a fake rat?" a boy Caroline didn't know asked rather loudly. "Next time maybe someone should try a rubber chicken—you know, like they sell in joke shops for the little kids."

A ripple of laughter erupted. It suddenly occurred to Caroline that she and Micah were probably not the only students at Pinecone Arts Academy who resented Marissa and her meanness.

"Shut up, Dylan," Marissa said. But her voice was so thin that Caroline thought it might evaporate.

"Enough," said the teacher. "Everybody, return to your tables for now. If you know anything about this, tell me. This is not funny. There will be consequences for this behavior."

Caroline gulped—but next to her, Micah grinned. Widely.

CHAPTER TWENTY-FOUR:

IN WHICH THE INVESTIGATION TAKES AN UNEXPECTED TURN

LOCATION: Bedroom, 9:00 p.m. last night

EVENT: C. had red paint stains on her hands. Just red.

QUESTION FOR FURTHER INVESTIGATION: Why?

Something was weird about Caroline again. Lara knew it. And so she watched her sister very, very carefully throughout the entire day. Even now that school was over, she tried to keep an eye on Caroline. Sneakily, of course.

An uncomfortable silence lingered between them as they waited for Aviva by the entrance. It was not for lack of trying on Lara's part. Yet Caroline kept responding to her inquiries with one-word answers. How very annoying!

"Ahem."

Lara glanced up to find Principal Jenkins. At first, she tensed. Was she in trouble? She hadn't done anything wrong lately! At least, not as far as she could remember.

Then she realized: Principal Jenkins wasn't talking to

Lara. Her scarily serious look was directed at Caroline.

"Miss Finkel," she said. "I would like to talk with you in my office."

In no time at all, Caroline's face became a particularly unhappy shade of pale. Lara squeezed her on the shoulder. Sure, her sister was so obviously hiding something. But that did not mean Lara was about to allow Principal Jenkins to do . . . whatever it was she was planning to do.

"If Caroline goes, I go," she said.

Principal Jenkins nodded. "That really is not necessary. Your sister is not in trouble. But if it would make you feel better . . ."

"It would."

Without her tablet in hand, Caroline remained silent. Lara straightened her back as they walked into the office. She could totally handle this.

Principal Jenkins gestured for them to sit down in the squishy chairs across from her desk. Lara sank into one and tried to keep her focus. She would not be lured into complacency, and she intended to let Principal Jenkins know it.

"If you don't follow the Americans with Disabilities Act, I am going to let our lawyer know about it," Lara informed her.

The Finkels did not actually have a lawyer. But Principal Jenkins didn't need to know that. The principal sighed and looked at Lara.

"Neither of you is in trouble," she said. "I just wanted to have a talk with Caroline."

Lara did not relax a single millimeter, and neither did her sister. She crossed her arms across her chest but did not speak.

The principal focused her attention on Caroline. "I understand that you've made a new friend . . . Micah Perkowski, is it?"

Ah. So that was the boy Caroline sent thirty katrillion texts to every day. The boy who had done something or other with fake blood, even if Caroline wouldn't admit to anything. Lara immediately disliked him.

Hands shaking, Caroline pulled out her tablet and started to type. "Yes," she said.

"I am glad to see you make friends," Principal Jenkins said. "Although I wonder if perhaps he is not the best choice."

Caroline's fingers flew across the screen. "He is a very good friend to me."

"Okay. However, I do have . . . questions. I'm sure you know what happened at lunch today."

Lara scrunched her face into a frown. School gossip rarely reached her, let alone sixth-grade gossip. But even she had heard about some unusual events. Something involving a screaming girl and a lunch box and a dead rat that was neither dead nor a rat. It all sounded rather bizarre.

Of course, it was ridiculous that such a thing could be at all connected to Caroline. And yet Lara could not help but recall the Mystery of the Red Paint.

At first, Caroline didn't respond to the principal. But Lara could practically feel her muscles tense up. Maybe it was sisterly psychic powers. Maybe it was just that she knew Caroline so well. Whatever the cause, she just knew that her sister was heading toward a very bad place.

Lara should do something. Protect Caroline now, get answers from her later.

"I don't think my sister had anything to do with that dead rat. Or whatever it was. You don't know her like I do," Lara insisted.

Unless I don't know her as well as I thought, a voice in Lara's head whispered.

Principal Jenkins looked at her with pursed lips. "I'm not accusing Caroline of anything. I'm sure she didn't have anything to do with the incident. I've been talking to her art teacher, though. And I was wondering if perhaps any of Caroline's new friends might have been involved."

Obviously she meant Micah. Lara tapped her fingers against her leg and thought about it. She didn't know very much about this Micah character. But just last week, he'd been running around with fake blood. Perhaps he really was just the sort of little jerk who would go around putting fake rats into people's lunch bags.

Caroline typed at top speed. "You have no proof that Micah did anything," she said. As soon as she was finished, she started glaring at the stapler on Principal Jenkins's desk. It was a very impressive glare.

Principal Jenkins gave a not-really smile. "I don't claim to know what happened. But your art teacher did mention her suspicions about your friend. She said that just last week, there was an incident. She thought Micah might be involved."

Lara could feel Caroline shake next to her, just like when they were little and used to huddle together during a particularly scary rainstorm.

"Can't you see you're upsetting my sister?" Lara asked.

"I apologize," Principal Jenkins said in a not-sorry voice. "But I do have to know these things."

"Micah didn't put the rat in Marissa's lunch box," Caroline said finally.

As always, her British computer voice gave nothing away. But Lara couldn't help but wonder. Caroline had been awfully careful with her words. Too careful.

Principal Jenkins looked most unhappy—a fact that pleased Lara more than it ought to. "Well. If you say so . . ." she said.

"I do."

Time to put an end to this interrogation session. If anyone was going to interrogate Caroline on this subject, it would be Lara.

She stood up and placed her hands on her hips. "My sister doesn't know anything. Can we go now? Our cousin is waiting for us."

Principal Jenkins sighed, but at last she nodded. "Well. Please do let me know if there's something else you'd like to share with me," she told Caroline.

"Sure," Caroline said. Lara almost snorted.

Lara's head spun in a thousand different directions as she escorted Caroline out of the office. Something about the whole thing just seemed, well, suspicious. Georgia Ketteridge would say that it reeked like bad ham on Christmas. Lara had no personal experience with bad ham, or Christmas, but she imagined that such a thing really would reek.

She replayed Caroline's words in her head. Micah didn't put the rat in Marissa's lunch box.

All at once, Lara remembered something. Last night, she'd wanted to play with Kugel. But she couldn't find any of his mouse toys anywhere. Now, that was hardly unusual. Kugel was notoriously good at losing toys. Ima always threatened to stop buying them for him, but he got away with such irresponsibility on account of being so cute. And also a cat.

Then, of course, there had been Caroline's paint-stained hands. Her very obviously red hands.

Maybe it meant nothing. Yet when she considered the fact that some sixth-grade girl found a not-dead not-rat in her lunch . . . maybe it did mean something.

Lara gulped. Caroline had said Micah hadn't put the supposed rat in the lunch box. Perhaps he hadn't.

Perhaps Caroline was the one who committed the crime.

It was the first night of Rosh Hashanah, so Lara probably should have gone to services at synagogue. Should have— but she didn't. Given her current mood (very bad), she'd asked Ima if she could stay home. Ima must have been in no mood for an argument, so she agreed. Caroline, too, stayed home. That gave Lara plenty of time to observe her sister and to stew.

The idea that Caroline would place a fake dead animal in someone's lunch was completely ridiculous. Caroline! And yet the more she thought about it, the more sense it made.

She had to know for sure. Could she somehow weasel a confession out of her sister?

Lara considered taking the direct approach. She could just ask, "Caroline, did you paint one of Kugel's toys to look like a dead rat and then put it in a girl's lunch box? And also, why?"

But as much as Lara liked the idea of a direct approach, she suspected that it might not work. Whenever Georgia Ketteridge wanted to question an unsuspecting witness, she was sneaky about it. Subtle. Lara would have to be too.

She certainly couldn't count on Caroline to tell her the truth on the matter. No, she needed more evidence. And when she spotted Caroline texting rapidly over dinner—again—she knew exactly what she needed to do. Whatever it took, she would get her hands on that phone.

Caroline was a girl who liked her routine. Every evening at eight, she took a bath for about twenty minutes. For Lara's purposes, that should be enough.

She waited until she heard the steady stream of water pit-patting from the bathroom. Then she made her move.

Lara's heart pounded as she grabbed Caroline's phone off her nightstand. She got the PIN right on the first try, because of course she knew Caroline's favorite numbers. And there it was. Everything she needed to know was right there.

As she opened up Caroline's text messages, it occurred to Lara that she ought to feel guilty. Did she feel guilty?

No, she did not. Besides, Caroline could be in real trouble. It was practically Lara's obligation to figure it all out.

Lara glanced at the messages. Caroline really only texted one person: Micah.

There were far too many messages for Lara to read. It didn't matter. She only needed to look at the most recent texts. Once she did, the story was very, very clear.

Great job! Micah had written several hours previously. *That mouse toy really did look like a dead rat.*

Lara mentally awarded herself a point for having solved the mystery. Then she frowned. She'd known that Caroline had been more distant ever since school started. But this . . . this was something else entirely.

Sweet Caroline, with her art and her Candy Crush obsession and her general sensible-ness. The same girl who was, apparently, playing cruel tricks on her classmates.

It was confounding.

Maybe Lara didn't understand her sister as well as she thought. Still, she felt quite certain that her sister wouldn't do something so cruel without good reason. Whoever this girl was must have deserved a scare. Who could it be?

It did not take much detective work to land upon an answer: the girl who had destroyed Caroline's sculpture, back on the first day of school. That had to be it.

Well, Lara certainly couldn't object on moral grounds. In her opinion, that girl deserved at least a dozen fake dead rats, plus some dead possums and squirrels thrown in.

No, that wasn't the trouble.

But why had Caroline turned to this Micah boy for help when she refused to talk about it with Lara? Her very own sister!

As Lara quickly scrolled through dozens of messages between the two, she couldn't help but wonder. Had she been . . . replaced? By a boy who wore X-Men T-shirts and had a bizarre obsession with fake blood?

For the next several minutes, Lara continued to stare at the phone screen. Only when the sound of the bath draining water began did she put the phone back where she'd found it. She certainly didn't want Caroline to know what she'd done. Still, she couldn't let the issue rest.

Lara and Caroline would most certainly be having a conversation. Soon.

Although she was bursting with the desire to unleash all her questions right away, Lara chose her moment carefully.

She waited until right before bed, when Caroline was brushing her teeth. Lara figured that her sister was probably on the groggy side so close to bedtime. Besides, she couldn't run away when her mouth was still full of peppermint-flavored toothpaste.

Lara did not knock on the bathroom door. She just let herself in.

"Hi, Caroline!" she said.

Caroline did not answer on account of her hands being occupied with toothbrushing. Her eyes narrowed in a definite glare and Lara's heart thumped faster.

"That meeting with the principal was really terrible, wasn't it?" Lara asked. Softening her sister up with sympathy seemed like a good tactic.

There was no answer, of course. But Lara was pretty

sure that her sister started brushing with enough vigor to make her gums bleed.

"I wonder why she thought your friend was involved in the whole dead rat incident," Lara continued. "I don't know him well, but it doesn't seem like something a friend of yours would do."

Caroline finished brushing. She rinsed her mouth. Finally, she picked up her tablet and responded.

"He is really nice," she said.

Lara immediately noted that Caroline hadn't really addressed the issue of whether or not Micah was the kind of person who would stick fake dead rats in people's lunches.

"I'm sure he is nice. And that girl—well, I don't know very much about the sixth graders. But I bet she's a real nightmare. Personally, I don't think it's wrong to play a little trick on that kind of a person. When you go around acting the way she does . . . well, that's the kind of thing that happens, isn't it?"

For a long time, Caroline did not respond. Lara quirked an eyebrow at her.

"I guess," she said finally.

"Mmm," Lara replied. "Just so you know, if you do know anything about what happened . . . you can tell me.

I promise I won't tell Ima or Principal Jenkins. Especially not the principal. I don't care to spend any more time in her office than absolutely necessary."

There it was. An invitation for Caroline to tell Lara everything, with the promise that nothing bad would happen if she did. Now the only question was, would she accept it?

"Mind your own business, Lara," Caroline said.

Then, nothing. Caroline just picked up her tablet, marched out of the bathroom, and crawled into her bed without saying so much as a good-night.

It was all Lara could do not to scream out loud. She'd given her sister every chance to tell the truth. They could have been Lara-and-Caroline again. Instead, Caroline had told her not to bother. Apparently, she didn't need Lara anymore. Not when she had Micah Perkowski.

Fine. From now on, maybe Lara didn't have to try so hard to be a good sister.

She mentally composed another entry in her notebook.

PROBLEM: *I'm not Caroline's best friend anymore.*

CHAPTER TWENTY-FIVE:

THE CASE OF THE NOT-SO-HAPPY HOLIDAY

LOCATION: *The usual, dinnertime, blah blah blah*

EVENT: *Rosh Hashanah stuff is happening. I don't feel like writing anything else.*

In theory, Rosh Hashanah was a moment for celebration. So, despite her decided lack of holiday spirit, Lara went about the usual Rosh Hashanah business the next morning. She dressed up in her very nicest dress for synagogue—purple with white trim. She went to synagogue and recited the prayers. She mostly contained her rage at Benny, who had taken to blowing the shofar at inconvenient moments.

By the time the late afternoon rolled around, Lara just wanted to curl up in bed with a book. Unfortunately, reading wasn't generally considered an appropriate Rosh Hashanah activity.

"Hello."

Lara glanced up at her sister, who was dressed in a bright green dress that Lara considered rather hideous. "Hi," she said.

"We're going to Lake Sammamish to do tashlikh. Do you want to come?" Caroline asked.

Lara made a face. She did not particularly want to walk around the lake in the cold while throwing bread crumbs into the water. The ritual of tashlikh was supposed to symbolize throwing away sins for the new year, but Lara didn't feel particularly burdened by sin. Caroline, however, probably could do with throwing several loaves into the lake. She could do that without Lara, though. Just like she did everything without Lara these days.

She shrugged. "No thanks."

For a moment, Caroline looked as though she was about to say something. Instead, she just said a single word. "Fine."

Lara wandered into the kitchen in search of something more interesting to do. Instead, she just found the chaotic sight of her father and Aunt Miriam trying to cook at the same time in the same kitchen. Well, hopefully at least one of them would manage to cook decent food.

She returned to her room to enjoy a precious few

hours of quiet time before the holiday started up again. Sure enough, Ima called the family to dinner at exactly six o'clock.

"When can I have my shofar back?" Benny asked Ima.

"Yom Kippur. Possibly," their mother replied.

Lara silently cheered the apparent confiscation of Benny's shofar. No doubt he'd find some other way to annoy her, but she would take the victory.

She slid into her favorite seat at the dining table. A few moments later, Aviva joined her. Lara reminded herself that she was trying to be nice to Aviva now. Maybe it could even be her Rosh Hashanah resolution. After all, Aviva actually wanted Lara's friendship. Unlike certain other people.

"L'shana tova," she told Aviva. There. Wishing her cousin a good year was, at the very least, a start to her new and improved approach.

"Thank you," Aviva said. "But you should know that it's not actually 'l'shana tova.' It's just 'shana tova.'"

Clenching her fists, Lara sighed. Already she regretted her choice of resolution. Maybe she should just pick something easier, like cleaning her room more often.

"Why exactly is the *lah* wrong?" Lara asked crossly. She'd always rather liked the sound of the Hebrew *lah*, and not just because it sounded a little like the first syllable of her own name.

"*Lah* means 'for' in Hebrew. So if you say 'l'shana tova', you're saying 'for a good new year.' That sounds a little odd, do you not think so?"

Lara bit her tongue. Several sharp retorts popped into her brain, most of which centered around Aviva's problems with English. She did not, however, actually say any of her mean thoughts. Really quite noble of her, when you thought about it.

Still, she wasn't going to let Miss Know-It-All have the last word.

"I don't see why saying 'for a good year' is wrong," she said. "After all, we say 'l'chaim.' That means 'for life,' doesn't it? Isn't that the same thing?"

Aviva bit her lip and looked down at the plate setting of Ima's best china. "I don't know. It's just that I've never heard a Hebrew speaker say 'l'shana tova.' I just thought you'd want to know."

"Well, I don't," Lara said, more sharply than she'd intended.

The rest of the family bursting in for dinner spared Lara from the need to continue the conversation. Thank goodness.

Lara glanced at Caroline. She opened her mouth to invite Caroline to sit next to her. Before she could manage to find the right words, Caroline found a seat at the other end of the table.

Fine.

Aunt Miriam came out, hands full of platters. Lara's mouth watered in anticipation.

"*Anyada buena, dulse i alegre,*" Aunt Miriam said from the head of the table.

Lara blinked in confusion. Those words weren't English, obviously. But they didn't sound like Hebrew, either. If anything, it sounded a lot like Spanish, which was most definitely not Lara's best subject.

"What does that mean?" Benny blurted out.

"It's Ladino," Aviva answered for her mother. "It's our New Year's greeting. The Sephardic greeting, I mean."

Lara scowled. She and her siblings were Sephardic too, even if Dad wasn't. There really was no end to Aviva's know-it-all-ness.

Aunt Miriam nodded. "Yes. And in the Sephardic tradition, we're going to have some *yehi ratzones*—appetizers, that is—before our dinner."

"Oooh, mozzarella sticks?" Benny asked. "Nachos?"

"Not exactly," Aunt Miriam replied.

Yehi ratzones turned out to be decidedly less appetizing than nachos. Still, Lara was hungry enough to manage a few baked apples and a spoonful of spinach. Soon enough, the main course would be out. She hoped.

"I hope your dad cooked good food this time," Aviva said, dipping an apple into honey.

"Of course he did," Lara snapped. After all, Dad had made plenty of great food since the brisket fiasco. "I hope you actually can appreciate it."

"Stop, Lara," Caroline said—the very first words she'd said directly to Lara for the entire dinner. "Aviva didn't mean anything by it. You don't have to get so mad over every little thing."

Lara glared. Just as she was busy coming up with the perfect response, Dad plopped a plate of roast chicken onto the center of the table. Lara grabbed a leg and was relieved to find that it tasted just as it ought to—juicy, moist, with just a hint of rosemary.

For several blessed moments, they enjoyed the satisfaction of good food. There were no whining comments from Benny, no know-it-all lectures from Aviva, no reprimands from Caroline. It was, Lara decided, a Rosh Hashanah miracle.

After finishing her second drumstick, Lara pulled out

her notebook. With so many bad things to record lately, it was nice to report on something happy.

Noah—noisily chewing on sweet potato kugel next to her—peered over her shoulder. "What's that?" he asked, not bothering to swallow before speaking.

Lara wrinkled her nose at him and set down her notebook with a thunk. "That's none of your business. But it just so happens to be my detective notebook."

Her brother smacked his lips together noisily. "You're still doing that? What are you working on now—a mystery involving cat vomit?"

Clenching her fists, Lara gave Noah her very meanest glare. "As a matter of fact, I have uncovered quite a bit of information. Information that might interest you, in fact."

His eyebrow quirked. "Oh, really? Well, I'd love to see it, in that case."

What happened next happened quickly. Far, far too quickly. Noah reached over Lara's half-empty plate—so rude!—and grabbed the notebook. He started flipping through the pages at a rapid speed.

"Give that back!" Lara protested.

"Noah, give your sister her notebook back," Ima said, using her Ima-est voice.

Noah looked Lara straight in the eye, shut the notebook, and passed it to her. That's when Lara knew. She just knew. It was too late.

"Some interesting stuff in there," Noah remarked. "You're quite the spy."

A hot, uncomfortable feeling invaded her body. What, exactly, had he seen? And would he keep his mouth shut about it?

Lara straightened her back and summoned her very best In Charge voice. "I am not a spy," she said.

Her brother only shrugged. "If you say so."

For a blissful moment it appeared as though that would be it. That somehow, miraculously, they could all just move on with the Rosh Hashanah dinner. They still hadn't started dessert, after all.

"You are too a spy!" Benny accused.

Well. So much for moving on.

Lara dropped her fork with a satisfying clang. She crossed her arms across her chest and turned to face Benny. "If that's what you want to call it, fine. By the way, have you given Ima her brooch back yet?"

For the first time in who knows how long, Benny became quiet. At least for a good ten seconds or so. Then he had plenty of things to say. "Lara, you said you wouldn't tell! You promised."

Lara certainly didn't like to think of herself as the sort of person who broke promises. But in that moment, she didn't much care. Besides, Benny had accused her of spying first. As far as she was concerned, that meant all promises were off.

Dad cleared his throat. "Uh, guys? I really don't think we should be doing this right now. Can it wait for another half hour, please? Probably less if we eat fast?"

Lara barely heard him. "Benny took your brooch and used it for his stupid invention!" she told her mother.

Ima rubbed her hand against her forehead. "Is this true?" she asked.

"Yes," Benny mumbled.

"We will discuss this—later." Ima placed an unmistakable emphasis on the word *later*. "For now, we will continue having a nice Rosh Hashanah dinner. As a family."

Lara privately thought there wasn't much hope for that, but she reached for her plate again. She picked at her kugel, barely tasting it.

Her family—well, some of them—tried. Aunt Miriam, who had missed some of the argument while tending to the pies—tried to engage Noah in conversation despite his obviously foul mood. "How are your college applications going?"

"Fine," Noah said. If anything, he looked even more miserable.

That gave Lara an idea. It definitely wasn't nice. But Noah hadn't been nice, either. Really, he'd started all of it. If not for him, this would have been a perfectly pleasant holiday dinner.

"Noah isn't going to college next year," she said.

"Lara, shut up," he said in an angry whisper.

At this point Ima's normally olive complexion had become a definite shade of red. She was, Lara thought, perilously close to spontaneous combustion. Or at least calling for a ban on all conversation for the rest of dinner.

Well, Lara would just have to say her piece now, then.

"Noah wants to go to community college and be a car mechanic. Right?" Lara said.

"What? Noah . . . is this true?"

Ima's voice was quiet—but deadly. Lara felt a vicious jolt of pleasure. That would teach her brother.

"Yeah, it is," Noah said. He seemed unable to look anywhere in particular. Lara suddenly felt empty. "That's what I want. But can we, um, discuss this later? Please?"

Ima did not respond. She did not even look up from her plate.

Just when Lara thought the meal would descend into

total silence, Aviva's thin voice piped up from her other side.

"I think being a car mechanic is an important job," she offered. "And also . . . Lara is being very rude. In my opinion."

As if her opinions meant anything! Lara felt the familiar rage return.

"Yes, let's hear all about your opinions," Lara said. "Actually, why don't you write them down? In English? Oh, right. You can't."

Some part of Lara knew that she was being horrible. Cruel. The very worst.

She ignored it. None of this was her fault. If her family didn't want their secrets revealed to everyone, then they shouldn't have been keeping secrets in the first place.

Right?

"Viva-la, are you struggling with English?" Aunt Miriam asked. "Why didn't you say something?"

At the same time, Caroline's computer voice sounded— loudly. She must have turned up the volume on her tablet. "Why do you have to be so horrible?"

The question was clearly directed at Lara. She bristled. For Caroline—of all people!—to scold her for horribleness . . . well, that hardly seemed fair.

"I'm just telling the truth," Lara said. Her voice was as firm as she could manage, and that was very firm. "It's not like I did something really horrible. Something like putting a fake dead rat in a girl's lunch box, for example."

"Lara, I don't know what you think you're doing, but you need to stop. This is not the time and place," Ima said. She seemed to have recovered from her shock.

Lara glared. "Come on! Aren't you even going to ask about the fake dead rat?"

"A fake dead rat sounds cool," Benny commented. "Though not as cool as a real dead rat."

Ima pushed away her plate and folded her arms across her chest. "There will be no talk about dead rats, real or otherwise, at this table."

A long stretch of silence wrapped around the room. Suffocating it.

Then Caroline spoke.

"Lara's right," Caroline said. "I did something bad. With a fake dead rat. I don't know how Lara found out."

Eyes narrowed, Lara turned toward her sister. "Like that even matters! You did something horrible."

Dad dropped his cup of soda, causing shards of glass to shatter all over the floor. He let out a sound that was half choke and half hiccup. "Lara," he said after recovering. "Maybe it's time for you to take a break. How about you go someplace quiet?"

If Lara hadn't already been well and thoroughly mad, that would have riled her up plenty. Why was she the one being scolded like a child and told to go away when Caroline was the one who had broken the rules? It wasn't fair. Nothing about this was fair. So the words continued to spill out of her mouth before she could think too much about what they meant and whom they hurt.

"Take a break? You mean like you took a break from work because you couldn't do your job right?" she asked. "No thanks."

Her words were mean. Lara knew that. But they also happened to be totally and completely true. There couldn't be anything wrong about that, could there?

"Sheesh," Noah muttered next to her. "You so need to learn when to quit." Lara ignored him.

But the pinched, lost look on Dad's face . . . Lara could not ignore that. The moment she saw it, she realized what she'd done. And the weight of it became impossible to bear. She wanted so badly to run away—away from the dinner, the house, and life in general. Of course, she couldn't. She couldn't even move from her chair.

Ima closed her eyes. No one else said a word. "Perhaps we just should not talk until dinner is over."

Nobody objected.

Lara finished every morsel of food on her plate. She tasted none of it.

CHAPTER TWENTY-SIX:

THINGS SAID,
THINGS UNSAID

Not yelling at Lara required every bit of self-restraint that Caroline possessed. Even then, she felt a scream rise up in her throat—not a computer-voice scream, but an actual scream.

She resisted the urge, barely.

She probably deserved it. For all of Lara's cruelty, she hadn't actually said anything that wasn't true. Caroline really had done a horrible thing.

Of course, her sister had been horrible too—not to Caroline, perhaps, but to Noah and Benny and Aviva and especially Dad. She had no idea what had come over Lara, nor did she care. Too many feelings swirled up inside Caroline's chest. She could not keep track of the colors and shapes that streamed through her mind.

Although it seemed impossible that the horrible dinner would ever end, it did. Caroline offered to help clean up, but Ima shot that idea down in the space of approximately two seconds.

"You need to talk with me and Dad," Ima informed her. "Your sister can help Aunt Miriam clean up."

Lara nodded, and shot Caroline a look. Which Caroline ignored.

Caroline's whole body trembled as she walked toward the living room, where Dad and Ima awaited her. Trouble—real, honest-to-goodness trouble—had always been something other people suffered through. Usually that person was Benny, or occasionally Lara or Noah. Now? Caroline was facing nothing but trouble, all on her own.

And as much as she wanted to blame Lara, she knew the biggest mistake had been hers.

She sank into the couch and waited for her lecture.

"I think we can all agree that tonight has been very . . . eventful," said Ima. She looked as though she'd just swallowed several pieces of Dad's gross brisket.

"That's one word for it," Dad muttered under his breath. He still looked out of sorts. Caroline longed to hug her father, to comfort him, but she wasn't sure she could stand being touched at the moment.

Ima cleared her throat. "Caroline, please explain this rat incident."

Caroline stared at the screen of her tablet. She needed to start giving it words, explanations, something that would somehow make Ima's lips un-purse themselves.

The blank screen stared back, taunting her.

Dad squeezed her shoulder in a surprising comfort. "Maybe you should start at the beginning," he said softly.

She supposed that made sense. And so Caroline began to type.

She tried to explain. About Marissa and Helena the zebra and Micah and everything else. Tapping all of that out letter by letter took a lot of time. Finally, Caroline finished. She pressed "speak" on her tablet, and she waited.

As her computer voice spoke, Caroline stared into the swirly flowers on the pillow she cradled in her lap. It was certainly easier than looking at Ima or Dad.

". . . so that is what happened," the computer voice concluded.

Nobody spoke, though Ima let out a sigh. Caroline bounced in her seat.

To her surprise, Dad was first to break the silence. "Well, Lina-Lin, that's quite the pickle you've got yourself into," he said. "I have to admit that I did not see this coming."

Caroline glanced up to see that her father was fighting back a grin. Now that certainly was an unexpected development.

"Joseph, this isn't funny," Ima said in a very Ima-like voice. "You could have done a lot of harm to that girl, Caroline. And I really don't know how I feel about you being friends with this Micah boy."

This time, words came easily to Caroline as she typed. "Please please please don't make me stop being friends with Micah."

"We don't want to tell you who you should be friends with," Dad said quickly.

Ima grunted, but did not contradict him. The lump in Caroline's stomach felt just a little bit lighter. That had been one of her biggest worries—losing her friend. Her only friend, now that she and Lara were decidedly not on friend-like terms.

At least she had Micah, assuming that he still wanted to be her friend. Which, Caroline realized with a sinking feeling, was a rather large assumption.

"You must apologize to the girl, of course," Ima said. "I expect you to go and talk to Principal Jenkins about this and do whatever she feels is appropriate. In fact, I will accompany you for this talk."

Caroline tapped the "yes" button. There wasn't much else to say.

Ima reviewed the rest of Caroline's punishments.

She would not receive her allowance for the next month. She would, however, be quite busy cleaning out the garage.

"I imagine at least one of your brothers will be helping you out with that," Ima said dryly.

Right. With all of her own misery, Caroline had all but forgotten about Benny and Noah. But surely they were in trouble too—even if what they'd done didn't really compare to Caroline's mistakes.

A hot flash of rage rose up inside her, and try as she might, Caroline could not banish it. Why, oh why, had Lara been so horrible? Caroline would have liked to ask her, but that required talking to Lara. And that was something Caroline absolutely refused to do.

Ima was still talking, Caroline realized, but she only caught a word here, two words there. She could not concentrate well enough to arrange the sounds into sentences. Finally, Ima ran out of words.

"Can I go now?" Caroline typed.

Although her lips remained pursed, Ima nodded. "I suppose we've covered everything." Under her breath she added, "And we have several more conversations to get through this evening."

"Actually . . ." Dad began. "I have a question."

Caroline and her mother both stared at him. He had been remarkably silent through all of the scolding.

"I was just wondering . . . why did you do this, Lina-Lin?"

"I already told you," Caroline said. She had absolutely no desire to discuss this subject any further.

"Yes, I know. But is there something else, meydl?"

Caroline tapped the "no" button before Dad even finished the question. With barely a glance at Dad and Ima, she hurried out of the room. Away from her parents. Away from Noah and Benny, who paced by the door to the living room while Lara made sad faces.

Away from her sister.

*** * ***

LOCATION: *Dinner, Rosh Hashanah*

EVENT: *I messed everything up.*

QUESTION FOR FURTHER INVESTIGATION: *Is it even possible to fix my mistakes?*

Lara stared at the page, then glanced over at the door. There was still no sign of Caroline. She sighed and turned the page. Lara was rereading the third Georgia Ketteridge book—wait, no, it was the second—but couldn't follow the story. It didn't really matter. Georgia was, no doubt, doing something smart and awesome and inspiring. Something un-Lara-like.

She didn't even look at the book as she turned another page.

Finally, Lara couldn't take it any longer. She tossed the paperback on her nightstand and marched out of her bedroom. Her mission: finding Caroline.

She checked the living room—no Caroline. Then the den—no Caroline. Finally, just as she entered the kitchen, Lara caught sight of dark, curly hair.

Her heart sank. It was only Ima.

Ima turned around, cradling her favorite mug. "Are you looking for something? Or somebody?" she asked.

"She probably doesn't want to see me anyway," Lara mumbled.

Ima placed her mug on the table with a soft clang. "Yes, perhaps it would be best if you and Caroline had some time apart."

That was something Lara appreciated about her mother. No matter how bad things got, she never tried to deny that things were, in fact, bad. Lara thought that was something she and Ima had in common. Of course, Ima probably hadn't ever done anything like revealing everyone's secrets at Rosh Hashanah dinner. That kind of mess-up was purely Lara's territory.

"You're right," Lara mumbled. She shuffled away.

Lara had nearly left the kitchen when Ima's voice called her back. "She will forgive you."

"You really think so?" Lara allowed herself a tiny, tiny flicker of hope.

"I do. I have a sister too, you realize." Ima paused. "Of course, I cannot say how long it will take."

Well. That wasn't exactly a happy, uplifting thought. But it was something, so Lara tried to hold on to it.

"And Dad?" she pressed.

Ima gave a not-quite smile. "Your father loves you. No matter what you do."

Lara knew that already. But instead of making her feel better, it just made her feel worse. Her whole family loved her—she knew that perfectly well. And she'd repaid them with . . . *that*.

After mumbling her thanks to Ima, Lara wandered back to her bedroom. It remained empty. Even Kugel showed no inclination to stop by. Perhaps he too was taking Caroline's side.

The minutes ticked by, and bedtime crept ever closer.

For once Lara looked forward to it. Caroline would have to return to their room then, surely.

Lara picked up the Georgia book she'd dropped. She completed five chapters, though she didn't particularly enjoy them. All the while, she kept stealing glances at the door. The stupid, annoying, unmoving door.

With four minutes to spare, Caroline slipped in. Without offering a single look for Lara, she changed into her pajamas and tucked herself into bed.

Lara waited until the lights were completely out to speak.

"I'm sorry."

No response. Well, that made sense. Aside from the fact that Caroline was probably super mad—if one could put such a thing aside—Caroline didn't have her tablet out. So, obviously she couldn't respond.

The sensible thing to do, Lara thought, would be to just leave it at that. Maybe Lara's sorry-ness would somehow make an impression on Caroline as she drifted off into sleep, and she would wake up in a more generous spirit.

Of course, if Lara were in the habit of doing the sensible thing, she probably would not be in this predicament in the first place.

"I didn't mean to do . . . all of that," she continued. "I really didn't."

The sound of blankets shuffling came from Caroline's side of the room. Then, her computer voice.

"Be quiet, Lara," Caroline said.

For once, Lara was quiet.

CHAPTER TWENTY-SEVEN:

THE MYSTERY OF MISTAKES

LOCATION: Kitchen, breakfast time

EVENT: Everyone hates me.

No further investigation required.

Lara knew that her siblings could not possibly have held a meeting in the middle of the night, a meeting in which it was decided that they would not be talking to her for the next day. (Two days? A week? It couldn't possibly be more than a week, could it?) But it certainly felt as though such a meeting had taken place.

First, she tried making conversation with Benny. Lara figured that he couldn't possibly resist the opportunity to talk. And yet, resist he did.

"Are you playing any good video games, Benny?"

Nothing.

"How is your Rube-whatever machine going?"

Nothing.

"Do you want some of my hair clips for your machine?"

Still nothing. Honestly, Lara wouldn't have believed him capable of such a long silence.

Noah snorted. She glared at him, but her heart wasn't in it. *After all*, a voice whispered to her. *What were you expecting? For them to throw you a party?*

Aviva—of all people!—appeared to take pity on Lara. "It is so nice to be going back to school today, isn't it?" she asked, her voice squeaking.

"Not really," Lara said.

Even Aviva gave up after that.

Dad gave her a weak smile as he munched on his toast, but the attempt only made the boulder that had taken up residence in her chest even heavier. Truly, she would have preferred that he yell at her. That, at least, would have felt like a proper punishment.

After such a morning, Lara looked forward to school. At least at Pinecone Arts Academy she could be invisible as usual, instead of being the target of everyone's irritation. Right now, Lara welcomed invisibility.

Yet even school felt different. For one thing, both Dad and Ima drove the kids to school. Instead of just dropping them off by the curb like usual, Ima actually parked the car. She and Dad walked with Caroline to the front door, flanking her on both sides. Caroline fixed her gaze on her sneakers, and Lara could see that her hands trembled more noticeably with every step. Their destination was not a mystery.

Not your problem, Lara told herself. *Caroline can deal with it.*

Except that Caroline's problems kind of were Lara's problems too, weren't they? Caroline wouldn't be in this situation, being marched off to Principal Jenkins's office, if not for Lara.

Lara walked down the hallway. Past Principal Jenkins's office. Then she glanced back to make sure her family was nowhere in sight. And she promptly turned around.

As she lingered outside of the office, Lara did her best to appear as though she had a reason to be there. She dearly hoped that no one would question her. She didn't have a decent excuse. Or any excuse.

Now Lara needed to decide how close to the door she dared go. From her current position, she couldn't hear much of anything. The wooden door was awfully thick. Yet if she tried to creep any closer, she risked exposure.

As she slowly stepped toward the door, it occurred to Lara that she'd become rather familiar with spying ever since she started FIASCCO.

But this wasn't a FIASCCO mission. It was far too

depressing for that. Besides, Caroline was on the other side of the door. In a real FIASCCO mission, the sisters ought to be together.

Lara's face was just inches away from the door when she heard Ima's voice. ". . . thankful for your understanding, Principal Jenkins."

"Of course," the principal replied.

"Lara?"

She spun around to find Aviva, frowning as she clutched a piece of paper.

Lara leaped away from the door. She could not allow her parents and Caroline to overhear her and Aviva talking. She wasn't even supposed to be here!

"What are you doing here?" she asked Aviva once she felt sure they were out of hearing range.

"I am dropping off a note from my Ima explaining why I was absent on Rosh Hashanah," Aviva said. "Why are you here?"

"Same reason," Lara said.

Aviva cleared her throat, but did not otherwise comment on Lara's obvious lie. It was generous of her, really. Lara felt another pang of guilt as she remembered her harsh words: *Why don't you write it down? In English? Oh, right. You can't.*

Her cheeks flushed. Now, more than half a day later, it all seemed so absurd. Lara couldn't even remember why she'd been so angry in the first place. Not really.

With Aviva there, she couldn't really continue her spy-on-Caroline-in-the-principal's-office mission. She didn't really feel like it, anyway. So she waited as her cousin handed in her note.

"Can I ask you a question?" Lara asked as they left the office.

"You may," Aviva responded, because of course she would.

"Why are you being nice to me?" she blurted out. "After . . . you know, what I did?"

Aviva slowed her pace, but only slightly. "Because it's the period between Rosh Hashanah and Yom Kippur," she said after a brief pause. "It's important to use this time to reflect and start acting, well, better. For the new year."

She sounded as though a teacher at Hebrew school had called on her to explain the High Holidays, and yet still managed to seem completely sincere. Lara could not help but wince. Although she was not exactly an expert on the matter herself, she had to think that beginning the new year by being a mean blabbermouth was not exactly a positive sign of things to come. She supposed she just wasn't as good a person as Aviva.

"So, if it weren't for Rosh Hashanah, then you wouldn't be nice to me?" Lara asked.

"I don't know. Maybe." Aviva hesitated before speaking again, and when she did, her voice dropped in volume. "I hope I would still be nice to you. Right now you just seem so . . . sad."

Lara ground her teeth together. Caroline's anger toward her had been awful, but Aviva's pity just might be worse. Way, way worse. She considered walking away from her cousin right then and there. Of course, that would just add to the Terrible Things Lara Did list, wouldn't it?

"I have another question for you," Lara said in a rush. "Caroline and Benny and Noah . . . do you think they can forgive me?"

Aviva looked straight ahead. "I am not Caroline or Benny or Noah," she pointed out. "I can't really say what they think or feel."

It was just the sort of logical response she ought to have expected from Aviva. Lara sighed. She did not ask her cousin any more questions.

Yet as she went about her morning, the question continued to nag her. After much consideration, Lara only knew one thing for sure. If she were in Caroline's or Benny's or Noah's place, she wouldn't forgive her.

✱✱✱

Principal Jenkins peered at Caroline from behind her dark-framed glasses. Not a single muscle in her face twitched. Still, Caroline felt quite safe in her assumption that the usually unflappable principal was, in fact, flapped.

Ima could sense it too. "I understand that this was a major mistake on Caroline's part," she said. "She will, of course, accept any punishment that you think is appropriate."

Caroline tapped the "yes" button on her tablet for extra effect. She hadn't gotten much of a chance to talk thanks to Ima's long explanation of what had happened, but hopefully she managed to seem properly sorry.

The principal twirled a fancy pen in her hand and looked straight at Caroline. She willed herself not to run screaming from the room, however appealing such a move felt in this particular moment.

"The other day, when I called you into my office, were you lying to me?" the principal asked.

Caroline chewed on the insides of her lip with vigor

as she tapped the "yes" button once more. Both Ima and Dad winced visibly.

"I must say that is surprising," the principal said. "And disappointing, of course. Although I certainly understand wanting to help a friend."

Never before had Caroline seen Principal Jenkins so out of sorts. She would have been sorry for her, if she were not so distracted. It felt as though her insides were made of dry clay that might crumble at any moment.

Ima nudged her, and Caroline quickly tapped another button. This morning, she had programmed her app with several remorseful statements about the fake rat incident. At least she hoped that they seemed remorseful.

"It was my idea to play the trick on Marissa, not Micah's. I am very sorry for all of the harm I have caused."

Maybe it was silly. But Caroline wanted the principal to understand that it really had been her idea. Not Micah's. Hers.

"Yes. However, I cannot help but wonder. Caroline, would you say that Micah participated in the prank?"

Caroline hesitated. Of course Micah had participated in the rat prank. (And the other one, although Caroline had very carefully avoided discussing it.) Yet she sensed that Principal Jenkins was asking something quite different.

She squinted at the screen. Right now, all of the words and letters felt inadequate for the task of explaining, well, everything. In fact, Caroline was not sure she could explain any of it.

Tapping her fingers against the edges of the tablet, Caroline reminded herself to breathe. Then she typed.

"I did it," she repeated. "I painted one of our cat's toys to look like a dead rat. I put it in Marissa's lunch box during art class."

And there it was—a slight twitch on Principal Jenkins's face. Caroline could not begin to guess its meaning.

"Well, if that's your story, then there need to be consequences," the principal said after a too-long pause. "You will serve detention every day for a week. And, of course, you need to apologize to Marissa. It's acceptable to give her a written apology, given . . . everything."

Caroline tapped the "okay" button, but her thoughts certainly were not okay. One week of detention! It sure felt like a lot. But—and this was an important *but*—was it enough? Would a normal kid have gotten two weeks of detention? Possibly even a suspension? Caroline didn't know, and she didn't dare ask.

"Thanks for your generosity, Principal," Ima said. Dad nodded his agreement.

After Ima nudged her, Caroline began typing once more. "Yes. Thank you. I will not do anything like this again."

The principal smiled tightly. "I'm sure the next time you're in my office, it will be under much better circumstances."

As soon as Caroline left the office, Dad and Ima still glued to her sides, she began flapping her hands at maximum speed, letting out all of the emotions she'd been holding back in front of the principal. She supposed her confession had gone about as well as she could have hoped. But there were still so many uncertainties, especially the not-so-small matter of Micah's reaction. Had she just lost her only friend?

Caroline would have liked to talk all about it with Lara. But that was the one thing she absolutely could not do.

CHAPTER TWENTY-EIGHT:

THE MANY REGRETS OF CAROLINE FINKEL

Caroline spilled it all out the moment she saw Micah in art class. After she finished her explanation of everything that had happened, she stared at the tablet screen. Looking anywhere in the vicinity of Micah's face was entirely too much.

She could only hope he wouldn't hate her now.

He didn't respond right away, and Caroline could feel her heartbeat quicken. Then, he let out a most unexpected sound. A soft chuckle. "Wow, your sister is kind of the worst," he said.

After the events of the past day, defending Lara was just about last on Caroline's list of things she wanted to do. Still . . . this was Lara. Micah shouldn't be able to talk about her that way. She clutched her tablet tightly.

"She's not so bad." After she hit the "speak" button, Caroline realized that this defense might not be very convincing to Micah. She started typing again. "Well, she's usually not bad."

"You're such a nice person," Micah said. "If one of my brothers did this to me, I'd put salt and pepper in their cereal. Worse. I mean, I do that anyway."

Caroline squirmed in her seat. She was not a nice person anymore, she knew that perfectly well. Nice people did not put dead rats—or fake dead rats—into other people's lunch boxes. But she felt too exhausted to argue with her friend, so she did not say anything else. Besides, she figured that Micah would have plenty to say all by himself.

"Actually, there's an idea! Maybe our next prank can be on your sister. She's in seventh grade, right? Maybe we could rig her locker so that rotten fruit falls out when she tries to open it. Or . . ."

Micah went on for a bit, but Caroline did her best to tune him out. She didn't want to play a prank on Lara. She didn't know what she did want, exactly. But it definitely wasn't that.

Yet she didn't have the slightest idea of how to communicate to Micah without losing him altogether. And so, as he talked and planned and talked some more, Caroline said nothing at all.

Dear Marissa,
Caroline typed the words, paused, then sighed. Even

looking at them felt quite ridiculous. Despite her regret over the rat incident, Caroline certainly didn't think that Marissa was the least bit dear. But that was the right way to begin a letter, and Caroline knew she had to do this right.

She rubbed her eyes and continued to type.

I am sorry

No, that wasn't good. She went back and deleted. I am very sorry, she wrote. That felt better. Should she add another *very*? Or was that overdoing it just a little?

After five minutes of painfully slow writing, Caroline had only managed two sentences in total. Although Principal Jenkins had not specified how long her apology letter ought to be, she felt pretty safe in assuming that it needed to be considerably longer than that. Yet at her current rate, she'd be done with middle school before managing to complete the letter.

Caroline leaped up from the computer and paced back and forth, back and forth. Maybe she was going about this the wrong way. The blank screen irritated her, making it difficult to think. Perhaps she ought to write the letter by hand. If nothing else, it would be easier to fill up a page.

Yes, that was just the thing. She wandered downstairs in search of the perfect piece of paper. This was absolutely not a waste of time, Caroline told herself. Once she had the right paper, everything else would come into place. Then she could finish this ridiculous letter and continue on with her life, thank you very much.

She examined the different options in the Finkels' arts and crafts supply cupboard. After much consideration, she settled on a thick beige card stock. Caroline figured that a total snob like Marissa would probably like a letter on fancy paper. To the extent that she could like an apology letter for an incident involving a fake dead rat.

Caroline settled in the den with her fancy pens. Dear Marissa, she began, adding an extra flourish to the final a.

I am sorry for placing a fake dead rat in your lunch box. (Just so you know, it was not actually a rat at all. I put red paint on a toy that belonged to my cat, Kugel.) I should not have done this, and I am very sorry that you were upset.

A decent start, Caroline thought. She chewed on her pen and searched for additional words. There was still two-thirds of the page to fill.

"Art project?" Ima asked, wandering into the den with a vacuum cleaner in hand.

Caroline eyed the vacuum cleaner with suspicion. She preferred to be on a different floor whenever Ima decided to vacuum. Since Ima showed no signs of turning it on, it was probably safe to engage in conversation. She grabbed her tablet and began to type.

"I am working on my apology letter for Marissa," she explained.

"Ah." Ima pursed her lips together. "Well, I'm glad to see you work on that. Best to get it out of the way."

Caroline tapped the "yes" button, lacking anything else to say.

"Is the letter going well?" Ima asked.

Although Caroline considered simply tapping the "yes" button again, she hesitated. Ima would know it was a lie—she just had a way of knowing such things.

"Not really," Caroline said. "It's hard to say sorry."

Ima nodded. "That's certainly true. Have you considered asking your sister for help? She is good at writing."

Caroline typed her response quickly. "I know. But she is not very good at saying sorry."

There was no doubt about it—Ima winced. "I know things between you have been difficult lately, but I hope you can put it behind you."

Given her complete inability to come up with a nice-sounding response to that, Caroline decided not to say anything at all. She returned to her letter, because trying to be nice to Marissa in writing felt easier than trying to say anything nice about Lara out loud.

"I understand that she violated your trust."

Clearly, Ima wasn't nearly so willing to just let the subject go. Against her better judgment, Caroline went back to her tablet.

"It's not just that," Caroline said. "She hasn't even tried to say sorry."

"Well, have you given her a chance?" Ima asked.

Why did Ima have to be so very reasonable all the time? Ever since that night, Caroline hadn't allowed herself to spend more than a few minutes in Lara's presence. Whenever her sister tried to speak, Caroline immediately put away her tablet.

"I haven't really talked to her much," Caroline admitted.

"That might be your first problem right there," Ima pointed out. Of course she didn't say "duh" or anything like that, but Caroline felt that was Ima-speak for *duh*. "You know, my mother used to have these Ladino sayings that she liked to use. It was her way of teaching my sister and me important lessons, I suppose."

Ima rarely talked about her mother, who died years before Caroline was even born. Whatever this was, it had to be important.

"One of her sayings was, 'Quien quere a' la rosa, non mire al espino.'"

Although Caroline guessed that *rosa* meant "rose," she otherwise had no idea what any of it meant.

"It means 'If you love a rose, you must ignore the thorns,'" Ima explained.

Frowning, Caroline considered the matter. The idea of Lara being a rose seemed a little much, but okay. Suppose that her sister was, in fact, a rose. Caroline certainly loved her. But why should she have to ignore the rose's thorns—all the things about Lara that made her angry and exasperated and everything else?

"Thanks, Ima," Caroline typed. "That is very interesting. But I do not think that saying is true."

"Why not?" her mother asked.

Caroline thought about it. Finally, she answered. "When a rose pricks me, I can't ignore its thorns."

Ima rubbed her eyes. "I understand you feel that way now, but you won't always. You two will get past this."

"Maybe," Caroline said. *I hope so,* she added silently.

As Ima left, Caroline returned to her letter. Somehow, she managed to fill up three whole paragraphs describing how very sorry she felt.

She signed the letter in her prettiest handwriting.

Hopefully that would be enough.

CHAPTER TWENTY-NINE:

THE DAY OF ATONEMENT

EVENT: Nothing in particular.

QUESTION FOR FURTHER INVESTIGATION: What's the right way to say I'm sorry?

During the next week, Lara made it her mission in life to apologize as frequently and fervently as she possibly could. She apologized in speech. She apologized in writing. She even attempted an apology drawing, although that turned out so hideous that it needed to go straight into the trash. None of it seemed to affect Caroline in the slightest.

Her luck was a little better with her brothers. Benny, while not exactly happy with her these days, at least responded to her hellos and how-are-yous most of the time. Noah still refused to speak with her, but he'd stopped scowling. Well, mostly. It was something, Lara told herself.

Dad was Dad. He didn't say a single word about what

Lara had done, and she didn't dare bring the subject up herself. But a distinct feeling of uncomfortable-ness lingered between them, and so she found herself searching for any excuse to avoid her father. It was rather lonely. But it at least helped fend off the constant feelings of guilt.

Lara was beginning to think that perhaps the real mystery was how any family ever stayed together, when one mistake could so easily tear them all apart.

By the time erev Yom Kippur came around, the general mood in the Finkel house was approaching an all-time low. For the first time she could remember, Lara welcomed the prospect of spending a few hours in services at synagogue. At least she wouldn't have to deal with Caroline's quiet anger or Dad's emptiness or Ima's coldness.

Everything was not normal. Lara felt thoroughly tired of trying to pretend that it was. At least she wouldn't have to pretend to be happy on Yom Kippur.

The drive to synagogue was full of heavy silence. Finally, Ima spoke. "You girls have a choice. Would you like to go to the children's service with Benny, or the adult service with your father and me?"

"The adult service," Lara said immediately.

In truth, the children's service was probably—okay, definitely—going to be more fun. Even so, since Lara did not consider herself a child, she would not attend the children's service. She assumed that Caroline felt the same way.

Next to her in the back seat, Caroline clattered away on her tablet.

"The children's service," she said.

Lara's stomach twisted in a most unpleasant way. She could not help but interpret her sister's decision as a personal insult.

As the service began, Lara tried to put all Caroline-related thoughts firmly to the side. She stood up when the rabbi said to stand, and read along with the words in both Hebrew and English. Trying to figure out how much of the Hebrew she could read without looking at the English transliterations was a game of sorts, and one that Lara was quite good at.

When it came time for the Al Chet prayer—the special prayer for Yom Kippur—she recited the list of wrong-doings along with everyone else.

"For the sin we have committed before You by a haughty demeanor."

Lara winced. Had she been haughty? Probably.

"For the sin we have committed before You by the prattle of our lips."

Another wince. That one definitely applied to Lara.

"For the sin we have committed before You with proud looks."

Proud looks? Now that was just unfair! Honestly, it was almost as though this entire prayer had been written just to make her feel bad.

"For all these wrongs, we atone," the congregation chanted.

There! Lara had said the words. She'd tried to apologize to her family members approximately a bajillion times over the past week and a half. And now she'd atoned officially. That had to be enough, right?

A violin began to play. It started as a murmur of low notes, barely loud enough for Lara to hear from her spot in the twenty-third row. The instrument sang, reaching higher and higher notes. It was as clear as any member of the choir. A piano plunked along steadily in the background. Together, the music they made was the only sound in the entire sanctuary. Even the baby in the second row had stopped wailing. There was nothing aside from the song, slow and haunting.

It shook Lara to the core.

A few minutes, or perhaps a few hours into the song, the cantor chimed in. Lara recognized the song from other Yom Kippur services—"Kol Nidre"—though she could not say what a single word meant. At that moment it did not matter.

". . . sah-lach-tee kid'vorecha," the cantor concluded.

The spell lingered after the cantor's voice broke off, after the final note from the violin reverberated around the room. Lara stared at the words of her prayer book. Music rarely moved her, and prayer more rarely still. And yet there was just something about this song, sung in this way, at this very moment. It felt . . . well, Lara did not quite know what she felt.

More Hebrew chanting followed, but Lara did not read along in the prayer book. She stared ahead, as if the stained-glass windows of the sanctuary offered answers for what she ought to do next.

"Tonight we begin a very difficult job," the rabbi said. Lara squinted at the book, searching for the rabbi's words somewhere on the pages.

"FYI, this is the part where I begin my sermon," she said. "These words aren't in your books. And I'll try not to take too long. I know it's late and many of you aren't going to be able to eat or drink for the next day. Plus, the whole parking situation is bad. I get it."

Soft laughter rippled throughout the room. Lara

glanced at her watch, hoping that the rabbi's sermon really was short, or at least short-ish. That probably wasn't a very good thing to think on Yom Kippur. She just couldn't help it.

"So, every year we talk about atonement. Forgiveness. Doing better. And yet every year, we all fall a bit short. We all do things that we wish we could take back, if only we had the chance."

Lara could practically see the Rosh Hashanah dinner in her mind. She could feel the terrible words tumbling out of her mouth.

"But of course, we can't take things back. We can only try to atone. That's the entire purpose of Yom Kippur. So how do we do that, exactly? Well, that's where things get more complicated. I wish I could give you clear instructions, a recipe for how to get forgiveness. Unfortunately, no such magic recipes exist. Asking for forgiveness is hard work. And the person you're asking for forgiveness from has absolutely no obligation to give it to you. However much you might want it.

"We can ask for forgiveness on Yom Kippur, or on any other day. That's definitely a start. But getting forgiveness— really, truly getting it—is much harder than that.

"We need to show others why we deserve forgiveness.

And that's not something that can be done in a few words or a card. That requires ongoing action. It requires work. It requires us to think long and hard about the people we want to be."

More words came out of the rabbi's mouth—words about responsibility for one's actions. Showing empathy toward others. Willingness to change. After a while, it all kind of ran together in Lara's mind. She could only concentrate on one thing.

She had to get Caroline's forgiveness. No. She needed to earn Caroline's forgiveness.

As the rabbi concluded her sermon and the choir broke into the final song, Lara began to form a plan. It wasn't a perfect plan, to be sure. But she was going to give it her very best shot.

Lara knew exactly what she had to say. She'd repeated the words in her head for the last ten minutes, while she and her parents struggled through the rather large crowd. When they finally emerged, Caroline was waiting at the synagogue entrance. Lara took a deep breath and prepared for the big moment.

"I messed up. I shouldn't have been mean to everyone, and I definitely shouldn't have been mean to you," she began. "I don't entirely know how, but I want to make it up to you. I promise."

Caroline tapped her shoulder twice. It was her signal for "wait until my tablet is out and I can talk." Lara did not want to wait. Not even a little bit. But she owed it to her sister to try.

As soon as they arrived home, Caroline pointed toward the stairs. She wanted to talk. Lara didn't try to hide the wide smile that broke out on her face.

There were so many things she wanted to say, but Lara knew she should give Caroline the chance to speak first. She resisted the urge to peek at the screen as her sister tapped out her response.

"Are you just apologizing to me because it's Yom Kippur?" Caroline asked. Her computer voice pronounced the holiday incorrectly.

"No!" Lara insisted. Then she thought about it. "Well, the rabbi's sermon did make me think, but I'm not apologizing just because it's Yom Kippur! Come on, Lina-Lin, you know I've apologized to you about a bajillion times since . . . you know. Since I said all of those horrible things. I know it's not enough. But I want . . . I want to earn your forgiveness."

Caroline stared off into space for a bit. Then she began tapping once more. "Yes. And I want to forgive you. Really, I do. I know I'm not perfect. I have made mistakes too."

Lara quirked one eyebrow upward. She suspected her sister was referring to the fake rat incident. Lara very much wanted to hear that whole story. Undoubtedly it was quite interesting. But now wasn't the time. Now was the time to prove that she, Lara, was sorry. Super sorry. Super super sorry, even.

"So, do you accept my apology?" Lara blurted out. Okay, so maybe that wasn't the most subtle approach. After a week and a half of begging for Caroline to give her even a few measly minutes to talk, Lara wasn't terribly interested in taking the subtle approach.

"I guess so," Caroline said finally. "I probably didn't have the right to be so mad at you in the first place. It was my fault that I did the rat prank. You were just telling the truth. I deserved it. Although Dad and everyone else didn't."

"I know," Lara said. "I wish . . . I wish I could make it better."

Caroline did not say anything to that. Lara drew in a shaky breath and repeated her question for the millionth time. "Can you try to forgive me? For what I said to you, not for anything else."

Much to Lara's surprise, her sister's reply was quick. "Yes."

CHAPTER THIRTY:

THE CASCADE

LOCATION: *Bedroom, erev Yom Kippur*

EVENT: *C. forgives me.*

QUESTION FOR FURTHER INVESTIGATION: *Can everyone else forgive me too?*

Lara had thought that Caroline forgiving her—finally!—would mean a return to normal-ness. Or at least something close to normal-ness. Unfortunately, no such thing occurred.

It wasn't that Caroline was mean, exactly. Of course, even when they were officially fighting, Caroline hadn't been mean. She'd just avoided Lara at every possible opportunity. But now that they'd made up, Caroline showed little inclination to do any of the usual Lara-and-Caroline-type things—a fact that frustrated Lara.

Which was how she ended up spending Yom Kippur afternoon with Aviva, baking cupcakes. Well, Aviva did most of the actual baking. But Lara cracked eggs and stirred bowls at her cousin's instructions. Quite generously, she didn't even complain about Aviva being bossy.

Since it was still Yom Kippur, Noah and the grown-ups were nowhere to be found. They were fasting and didn't get to eat until sundown. Lara supposed all the cupcake smells were quite unpleasant to endure under the circumstances. Even if they would all be eating them later.

Next year, Lara realized, she and Aviva would be thirteen. That meant they would fast too. It all seemed so odd and adult-like. Lara wasn't at all sure she felt like an adult. Did adults make so very many mistakes?

At least Dad's absence from the kitchen meant that Lara could avoid the bad feelings that overcame her every time she saw him. She needed to apologize to him. She knew she did. If only she could figure out how.

Right as Aviva started taking the cupcakes out of the oven, Caroline appeared. In no time she was enlisted into decoration duty. To no one's surprise, her icing skills proved far superior to Lara's and even Aviva's.

Lara relaxed ever so slightly. Maybe everything wasn't quite back to the way it ought to be, but at least Caroline was okay being in her general proximity. That was a definite improvement over the previous ten days.

"That's a very nice tree," Lara told her, admiring her sister's cupcake.

"It's not a tree," Caroline informed her.

"Oh. What is it, then?"

Caroline did not respond until she had completed the cupcake. Now that the zigzaggy lines of icing were setting, Lara couldn't even guess what her sister had created.

"Nothing in particular. It's just a pretty pattern."

"Oh."

Since when did Caroline make drawings of nothing in particular? Probably around the same time she started playing pranks on people with her new friend. Lara tried to stop herself from frowning. But she could not stop herself from talking.

"I thought you forgave me," she blurted out in the midst of a rapidly failing attempt to make an icing-leaf.

"I did."

Lara knew she should just let it go. But after ten days of waiting to have a real conversation with Caroline, she wasn't in much of a letting-things-go mood.

"Well then why aren't you acting like it?"

"How am I supposed to act? I'm talking to you, aren't I?" Caroline said.

"Yes, but . . . ugh. I don't even know. Forget it."

Face uncomfortably hot, Lara concentrated on trying to salvage her now-lopsided leaf. Meanwhile, Caroline began a new cupcake without further comment. Lara could tell that Aviva was following all of it, but she didn't say anything either. Thankfully.

After they completed a full tray of cupcakes, Aviva got up and busied herself with cleaning the kitchen counters. She insisted on doing all of it herself because apparently Lara couldn't be trusted to use a washcloth without disrupting the "system."

And still Caroline did not speak.

Only the ping of Caroline's phone interrupted the silence. When Caroline glanced at the screen, she made a not-happy face.

"Who is it?" There was really only one person who ever texted Caroline, but Lara figured she should ask anyway.

"Micah."

Lara frowned. She had plenty of things to say about Micah. Of course she did. Still, right now she needed to be a good sister and earn Caroline's forgiveness. It was, perhaps, not the best time to unleash all of her Micah-related opinions. However justified those opinions might be.

"Are you still friends with him after, well, everything?" Lara asked.

Instead of answering the question, Caroline stared at her phone as though it might suddenly grow feet and start tap-dancing through the kitchen. She glanced at the screen but did not type a response for a good minute.

"Yes," she said finally. "At least, I think so. It's complicated."

Well, Lara had plenty of ideas for how to un-complicate the whole situation. Dumping Micah as a friend would certainly un-complicate things, would it not? But even though part of her really, really wanted to tell Caroline she ought to do just that, she stopped herself.

It was time to be advice-giving Lara, not opinion-giving Lara.

"Well, do you want to keep being friends with him?" she asked.

Caroline's answer came quickly. "Yes. I do. At least, I think so. But I don't want to keep doing mean things with him. I just want to text and sit with him at lunch and things like that."

"Then that's what you need to tell him. And if he's not okay with that, then good riddance to him."

There. Lara was pretty good at the whole advice-giving business, if she did say so herself.

Yet Caroline still looked doubtful. "It's not that easy.

I'm not like you. I can't just say what I want to say all the time. Even with my tablet."

Lara paused. Lately, her big mouth had caused catastrophe. Multiple catastrophes, in fact. Yet Caroline wanted to be more like her?

Well, maybe that was something for Lara to work with. An opportunity. Lara summoned every bit of confidence she possessed. She did her best to ignore the whispers in the back of her mind that Caroline didn't want her help. Would never, ever trust her again.

Because Caroline had forgiven her. And she was going to prove that she deserved it.

"Yes, you can. You can tell Micah exactly what you mean," Lara told her sister. "And I'm going to help you do it."

Caroline's face twitched, but then broke out into a smile. "All right then," she said. "Give me your lessons in being bossy."

✳ ✳ ✳

When Caroline returned to school after Yom Kippur, bright orange dots raced through her mind's canvas. No matter how she tried to force her thoughts into calm blues and greens, the awful orange kept coming back.

Lara grinned at her before they parted ways. "You nailed bossiness lessons and you're going to do great with that boy . . . I mean, with Micah."

Her sister was very clearly not a fan of Micah, but Caroline appreciated the effort nevertheless. She thanked Lara and went off to start her day. Throughout first period, Caroline kept replaying their bossiness lessons from the previous night.

"You can be plenty bossy," Lara had told her. "You tell ME what to do all the time!"

At first Caroline had protested. With the two of them it was always Lara who led Lara-and-Caroline, as she knew perfectly well. Lara came up with the big plans, and then Caroline helped carry them out. That was just how things were. And yet . . . maybe things could change. Maybe they had already changed. After all, Caroline had befriended Micah and pulled off two admittedly ill-advised pranks before her sister even discovered it. Now she just needed to find a way out, while still somehow managing to keep Micah as a friend.

She saw him for the first time in Experimental Art class. At the moment they were making sculptures out of recycled materials. Caroline still wasn't sure what she really wanted to do for the assignment, but Micah was quite enthusiastically stacking towers of bottle caps.

"I want to talk," she told Micah. That was exactly as she'd planned.

"Cool," Micah replied. He added another cap to his stack, which was now teetering rather perilously in his work space.

"Okay. Good," Caroline said.

Taking in a deep breath, she turned back to the tablet screen. There was so much she wanted to say. Lara would be able to find the rights words, she knew. She just needed to remember Lara's bossiness lessons.

She began to type.

"I like being your friend. But I don't like some of the things we've do—"

Before Caroline could finish typing the word *done*, a stampede of unpleasant sounds came. From the spot right next to her.

The strings securing Micah's bottle-cap sculpture had snapped, causing dozens of caps to scatter across the floor. With every *CLUNK* of a cap, Caroline felt her nervousness heighten. Her hands flew up to her ears to cover them, but it didn't do much good.

Things were too loud, too difficult, too everything.

She whimpered out loud and raced away from their table. It helped, but only a little.

Micah said a Very Bad Word. "Sorry, sorry!" he said. "I should have seen that this wasn't going to work. I didn't mean to upset you. Sorry."

Since Caroline had abandoned her tablet amid all the ruckus, she couldn't really respond. Not right away. She wasn't sure what she'd say anyway.

After taking a proper number of deep breaths, Caroline returned and helped Micah collect all of the bottle caps. Eventually things settled down to something that resembled normalcy.

She deleted the words she'd typed into her app and for the rest of the period, she said very little.

Lara would be so disappointed in her. She just knew it. What was worse, she was disappointed in herself.

CHAPTER THIRTY-ONE:

THE RIGHT WORDS

"So, how did it go?" Lara said. "Did you get to be properly bossy?"

Caroline winced. Her sister looked at her expectantly, hands flapping ever so slightly. For whatever reason, Lara obviously cared about the whole Micah situation. She'd gone out of her way to help, but now Caroline had to admit she'd failed.

"It didn't go at all," Caroline said shortly.

"What? Why not?"

Sighing deeply, Caroline tried to explain the whole bottle-cap situation as best she could. It wasn't a great excuse, she knew, but it was something.

As Caroline described the situation, Lara nodded. "Ugh, sudden noises." Lara shuddered dramatically. "I don't blame you for getting upset. I would have hated that too."

At that Caroline managed a small smile. Lara might be infuriating at times, true. But she still understood Caroline better than anyone else. She probably always would.

"I wish I had been able to say something to him," she

said. "But it was already so hard to find the words and then when the whole bottle-cap thing happened, I just felt so many different things and . . . I don't even know. It's probably stupid to get so upset by bottle caps."

Lara frowned at her. "It is not stupid. And we are going to figure out a way to solve the Micah Problem. I promise."

When Lara used *that* voice, there really was no talking her out of anything. And indeed, once they got home Lara plopped down in the den and immediately focused her attention on the Problem. (The way Lara said it, a capital letter was necessary, even in Caroline's thoughts.)

Caroline wasn't sure all of this would do much good. But she loved her sister for it anyway.

"We are going to figure this out," Lara insisted.

"Okay," Caroline said. She wasn't sure what else there was to say at this point.

Lara, of course, had plenty of contributions to the conversation. She flipped open her detective notebook, as if Caroline's inability to stand up to Micah was just another mystery in need of investigation. She scribbled something down in the notebook, then chewed on the cap to her pen.

"I have a question for you," Caroline blurted out.

"Hmm?" Lara looked up from her scribbling. "Yes?"

"Why are you working so hard to help me?"

At that, Lara finally put down her pen. "Are you saying that our sisterly bond isn't enough to inspire me to help you?" She stuck out her tongue. "Why, I am very nearly offended by that."

"I certainly don't mean to question our sisterly bond," Caroline said, repressing the urge to roll her eyes. "But why are you trying to help me? Lately you haven't been doing that very much at all."

All at once Lara's face became oddly serious. "Yeah. I know." She paused. "I guess after . . . everything that happened . . . I want to make amends. I want to show that you were right to forgive me."

"I appreciate the help. I do," Caroline said. "But I'm not the only one you need to make amends to, you know."

Her sister stared at her notebook page but didn't write anything down. "I know," she said in a quiet voice. "I . . . I wish I knew how to do the whole amends thing better. Especially with Dad."

Caroline could not help but think of her all-too-awkward letter to Marissa. The other girl had accepted it with a haughty sniff and shoved it in her backpack without a single glance. Honestly, Caroline could not blame her under the circumstances. There had to be a better way to say sorry than that, surely.

"I'll try to help you make amends," Caroline offered. "It's only fair, since you're helping me with Micah."

The beginnings of a smile popped up on Lara's face. "I think we have a deal."

∗∗∗

NEW MISSION: I will try to make amends with, well, every-one.

QUESTION FOR FURTHER INVESTIGATION: How?

When it came to Mission Make Amends, Lara decided she should start off easy. She figured that getting forgive-ness from Benny shouldn't be too difficult. And indeed, it was not. "I'm sorry," she told him. "Really, really sorry."

Benny shrugged. "It's okay. I shouldn't have taken Ima's pin-thingy. And it was mean for me to say that you're a spy. Even though you are."

"Not anymore," Lara said. "Promise."

And then she spent the next half hour watching Benny explain his zipper-zipping machine. By the end of it he was beaming and bouncing and being very Benny-like in general. Before leaving, she promised to be on the look-out for stuff he could use in future inventions. Stage 1: complete.

Noah wasn't too difficult, either. When Ima started nagging him to put in his college applications over dinner, Lara decided to say something. She might as well try to do good when getting involved in other people's business.

"I think it's cool that Noah wants to be a mechanic," Lara said.

Her brother looked surprised, but he smiled. "Thanks, Lara."

Dad agreed. "Ezter, we've discussed this. Can we maybe not get into it right now?"

Although she pursed her lips, Ima let the matter go. Lara counted that as having Made Amends to Noah.

Next up was Aviva. This time, she was sure to knock before entering Aviva's room. She entered to find Aviva sitting at her desk. A pencil was tucked behind her ear, brushing against her tightly woven braid.

"Hello," Aviva said. "Why are you here? Not that it isn't very nice to see you."

"I am here to make amends," Lara said. She might as well be honest about it.

Aviva frowned. "I think I know what that word means, but I am not entirely sure."

Right. Lara considered her predicament. Although she'd embarked on a mission that had *amends* in the name, she found it was rather more difficult to explain the word than she'd thought. Several moments of silence lingered as she tried to come up with just the right response.

"It means I want to say sorry," she said finally. "For being so mean to you at Rosh Hashanah dinner."

Her cousin gave her a tight smile. "It's all right. And you have already told me that you're sorry. This is the fifth time you've apologized to me."

Huh. Lara didn't realize that she'd apologized to Aviva quite so much. Now that the fact was laid before her, it all seemed a little pathetic. But this would be the last, most important apology. "Making amends isn't just about saying sorry, though. It's about showing that you're sorry. And I want to show you. So, uh, is there anything I can do for you? To show you how sorry I am."

Forehead creased in concentration, Aviva twirled one of her braids. Lara focused her attention on the twirling rather than Aviva's face. It felt easier, somehow.

"You are already helping me a lot with my writing in English," Aviva told her finally. "I think that is a good way to make amends with me."

Lara just barely restrained herself from letting out a frustrated grunt. Why did her cousin have to be so very nice about everything, to the point where she didn't even ask for a favor? Couldn't she see that Lara was trying to be good, or at least better than she had been?

"I can help you with your writing. Sure. But isn't there something else you want? Something else I could do for you to make up for everything?"

Aviva stopped twirling her hair. "Well . . . there is one thing."

"Yes?"

"I know we have not always gotten along. But I would like for us to try and be friends."

Lara stared. Of all the things she might have expected her cousin to say, she had not anticipated that particular request. And yet there was only one response.

"I would like that too," Lara said. She extended her hand and Aviva shook it.

In her mind, Lara checked Aviva off the list. Now only Dad was left.

Lara's skin heated up every time she thought about it. After what she'd done to Dad, how could she ever Make Amends?

✳✳✳

It turned out that Lara's solution to the Micah Problem was a good one. Now Caroline just had to do it.

You can, her sister's voice chanted in her ear. *Remember—we made a deal.*

Indeed they had. And Caroline intended to keep her end of the bargain.

When she walked into Experimental Art, she kept her back straight and her purpose clearly in mind. She took in one, two, three deep breaths while she walked over to her spot. Well, her and Micah's spot.

Micah usually rushed into class at the last possible second, but today he was already there, doodling on a piece of scratch paper. Was this perhaps a sign? And if so, of what?

Caroline had barely settled into her seat before pulling out her tablet. She opened up her speech app. But instead of going to the keyboard function, as she normally did, she cued up one of the speeches that she'd already written.

That had been Lara's idea. Since coming up with the right words at the right moment can be hard, Lara had pointed out, why not write the words ahead of time? The speech app was perfect for it.

And so Caroline tapped the first of her preprogrammed speeches. "I need you to listen to me."

Micah's eyebrow arched up in surprise, but he nodded. "Sure, Caro."

Caroline didn't feel much like Caro at the moment. But

then, Caro was Micah's friend who couldn't stand up to him. Today she had to be different. She had to be Bossy Caroline, as Lara put it.

Tapping her foot just a little bit, she pulled up the next speech:

"I like being your friend and I want to keep being your friend. But I don't like pulling pranks on people. It's mean and scary and it got me in trouble. I wish we could do things together that aren't just pulling pranks on Marissa or other people. Thank you for listening and I hope you still want to be my friend."

She had written the whole thing last night, doing her very best to select the right words. Although she'd considered making her explanation longer, ultimately she decided that this was enough. It had to be enough. Lara had given it her stamp of approval, after all.

Caroline listened to her own words and her leg-tapping intensified. This had to work and Micah had to listen to her. Didn't he?

Her computer voice stopped speaking, but Micah did not respond right away. He looked, Caroline had to admit, thoroughly confused by the whole thing.

"I thought you liked the pranks," he said. "My brothers and I always prank each other and it's fun."

This time, the right words came quickly. "I am not your brothers."

"Yeah, your hair is a little on the long side. Um . . . if I'm being honest, I didn't know you felt that way. Why didn't you say something sooner?"

Figuring out what to say next required all of Caroline's concentration, but she was ultimately pleased with what she came up with. "I didn't know how. Now I do."

"Okay," Micah said. He returned to his drawing.

Caroline frowned. What did he mean, okay? Okay, they were still friends? Okay, but I'm going to continue doing pranks anyway? She did not know and she did not like it.

"What do you mean? Okay what?" she pressed him.

"It's okay that you don't want to do pranks. But I do."

Then, nothing.

Caroline stared at her tablet screen and thought long and hard. Although she wanted to ask him if they were still friends, she did not. Lara's words came back to her. *If he doesn't want to be friends anymore, then good riddance.*

But . . . Micah had been a good friend, at least some of the time. They'd had their texts and their lunches and sitting together in art class.

It had been nice, having a friend.

An ache worked its way through Caroline's chest—small yet sharp.

It hurt. Part of her wanted to tell Micah that she hadn't meant it, that of course she wanted to continue doing stuff with him! Wasn't it worth it, if she could keep having him as a friend?

No. It wasn't worth it. Bossy Caroline knew what she wanted, and she'd said it out loud. She could not un-say it now. Sighing, Caroline picked up her pencil and returned to her sketch.

So, maybe she didn't have Micah anymore. But she looked around the room full of kids. Marissa and her friends were there, but they weren't the only ones. Surely someone else could be her friend. Someone who wouldn't ask her to do terrible things to other people.

She would just have to try again.

Caroline turned to the quiet girl who often sat across from her and Micah. They usually said hello, but rarely anything else. Maybe today could be different.

"Hi," Caroline said to the girl. "What are you making?"

CHAPTER THIRTY-TWO:

THE FINAL MISSION

MISSION MAKE AMENDS:
1. ~~Caroline~~
2. ~~Benny~~
3. ~~Noah~~
4. ~~Aviva~~
5. Dad (?????)

Lara looked over her list. At the very least, she felt satisfied-ish with her progress. After all, she had officially Made Amends with almost everyone.

But then there was Dad. Just looking at his name on her list gave her a mild stomachache.

Caroline peered over her shoulder. (Lara very nicely chose not to comment on her sister's poor manners. She was Making Amends, after all.) "You need to talk to Dad," Caroline informed her.

Lara frowned. Slightly. "I know that. I'm just waiting for the right opportunity."

That response merely earned her a Look from Caroline. She probably deserved it.

"Come on," Caroline prodded her. "I think he's downstairs right now."

Hands flapping at top speed, Lara searched for a good-sounding excuse for why she couldn't possibly talk to Dad at this very moment. The only thing she came up with was the rather queasy state of her stomach. But that wasn't really a good excuse, was it?

She considered Caroline. At the moment her sister was staring at her tablet, but Lara felt the weight of her gaze nevertheless. Her sister had stood up to the boy who was her only friend in the world, outside of their own family. From what Lara gathered, it hadn't gone too well. But Caroline stood up for herself anyway. That took serious bravery—the real kind, not the spying-on-your-family kind. Surely Lara could also be really and truly brave.

"Fine," she mumbled.

Finding Dad's precise location did not require any significant powers of deduction. The smells coming from the kitchen—cheesy, spinach-y smells—told Lara exactly where to find him.

Disrupting Dad when he was in chef mode was, generally speaking, a no-no. Maybe Lara should try again later.

No, a voice said in her head. *You have to do this now.* The voice sounded rather like Caroline's.

So Lara approached her father, words and fears and possibilities running through her brain like a bad headache.

"Oh, hi, Lara-bear," Dad said. He slid a dish into the oven and closed the door. "What brings you to these parts?"

"I'm making amends," Lara informed him. She couldn't think of how else to describe it.

"Ah." He leaned up against the kitchen counter, eyebrows furrowed together. "Well, I appreciate the gesture."

Dad started to wipe food-ish things off the counter. Lara supposed it was her turn to say something that was properly amends-worthy. If she could think of such a thing.

The oven hummed on in the background. Lara resisted the urge to peek inside. She picked up a wooden spoon that happened to be close by and began to twirl it—slowly at first, then more quickly. Finally, she willed herself to speak.

"I'm really sorry. I was really horrible at Rosh Hashanah. I shouldn't have said all of those things about you. I didn't mean them, honestly I didn't."

Her father squeezed her shoulder. "I love to hear that, Lara-bear. But I'm pretty sure you did mean it. Well, some of it, at least."

Lara's face heated. And she was pretty sure it wasn't because of her closeness to the oven.

"That's not true!" she insisted. "I don't really think that you're . . . those horrible things I said about you. I mean, you're my dad."

He nodded. "I know, honey. And I'm not saying that you think those things all the time. But I know I haven't been the best dad the past few months, ever since I lost my job."

Lara nearly dropped the spoon. She'd had this conversation in her head many times. So that she could plan out what to say. But never had any of those Dad-voices in her head admitted that he'd made mistakes.

Maybe she wasn't the only one who messed up sometimes. And maybe, just maybe, that was okay—so long as she could properly Make Amends.

"Obviously, the way you expressed your frustration wasn't great," Dad continued. "But I understand why you felt the way you did. And if you're asking for my forgiveness, well, you've got it, Lara-bear."

The bad feelings in Lara's stomach disappeared at once. Who knew that asking for forgiveness could be so very easy? And it felt good too. Very, very good.

Still, surely she had to do something else. Something more. Right?

"Thank you," Lara said. "So. What else do I need to do?"

Dad glanced at the oven timer, and then back at Lara. "Huh? I accepted your apology, hon. What else is there?"

Although Lara thought her meaning was obvious, she tried to find the right words. "I want to do something more than just say sorry. I want to show that I'm sorry. So that you know I mean it."

"I know you mean it. There's no need to go off on some mission to prove it. We're good, you and me."

Lara frowned. Now this was just too easy. Didn't Dad know that she had, in fact, established a mission to Make Amends?

"Come on," she pressed. "Isn't there something—anything at all—I can do to make things up to you? I'm really trying to make amends here!"

For a while, Dad didn't say anything. He continued wiping down the counter, even though it was already quite clean. "The garage," he said after wipe number four.

"What about it?" In the Finkel household, the garage was a place where things went, collected dust, and most likely were never seen again. Even Ima had long since given up trying to make the place orderly.

"You can help clean the garage. Your sister is already doing it as part of her punishment. You want to make amends, you can help her out."

Lara wanted to protest that she shouldn't have to share in Caroline's punishment. After all, she hadn't been the one to prank one of her classmates. But she'd asked for a way to Make Amends and her dad had given it to her. She couldn't very well complain now.

"Okay," she said. "I'll help Caroline clean the garage. We'll probably finish sometime within the next bajillion years if we really work hard at it."

Dad chuckled. "That's my girl."

Despite the humongous task before her, Lara smiled.

"Can I ask you something else?" she said. Dad seemed like he was in a good mood, so she might as well get all of her awkward questions out.

"Sure thing."

"Are you and Ima . . . okay?"

They definitely had seemed okay as of late. There hadn't been any fights, and on several occasions Lara had caught her parents looking at each other with one of those weird, kind of uncomfortable lovey-dovey looks. But still. She wanted to know for sure.

"Your mother and I are fine. We had a rough patch, and we're getting through it. That's what families do."

A wave of tension left Lara's body. Until that very moment, she hadn't fully realized that it had been there at all.

Just as Dad squeezed her shoulder once more, the oven let out a most obnoxious beep. Lara pressed her hands to her ears.

"That would be the spanakopita," Dad said. "It's done."

Lara perked up at the mention of one of her favorite foods. "You're making spanakopita? I thought you didn't know how to do that."

Her father grinned. "Well, that's why I'm going to learn. I wanted to learn more of your mother's family recipes. Plus, it's good practice."

"Practice for what?"

Dad opened the oven and carefully removed the tray. Lara's eyes widened at the sight of the golden brown, perfectly flaky pastry. She was pretty sure this particular culinary experiment could be deemed a success.

"Practice for when I go to culinary school," Dad said as

he set down the dish. "I'm starting in a few months, you know."

"You're going to culinary school? I didn't know that!"

This time, Dad's smile took on a decided cheekiness. "Well, Lara, I know you want to be a detective. But, believe it or not, you don't actually know everything."

"Right," Lara said, cheeks pink.

Well, perhaps not knowing things wasn't always the worst thing in the world. Good surprises were, in fact, rather enjoyable.

She marched over to the stairwell and called for her sister. "Lina-Lin! Come down! We have to clean the garage."

Her sister appeared moments later, forehead crinkled in confusion. "I thought I was doing that on my own."

"Nope. You're stuck with me."

Caroline smiled. "I guess I am. Let's get started."

ACKNOWLEDGMENTS

Writing this book has been a joy, and I absolutely could not have done it without the support of many, many people.

Thank you to my editor, Dana Chidiac. Working with you has made me a better writer. Lara and Caroline's story could not have come to life without your always keen insights. Another big thank-you to my agent, Jennifer Udden, who has helped me to handle the business side of publishing with deftness and humor.

I am fortunate to have the opportunity to work with a wonderful team at Dial Books for Young Readers and Penguin Random House. Thanks to the entire team: Lauri Hornik, Nancy Mercado, Regina Castillo, Tabitha Dulla, Mina Chung, Emily Romero, Christina Colangelo, Carmela Iaria, Debra Polansky, and their teams. A big thank-you to Kaitlin Kneafsey for everything you do to help my books find readers. A special thanks to Alexandra Bye for the beautiful cover art, and to Theresa Evangelista for your amazing design.

Thanks also to Joanna Volpe and the entire team at New Leaf Literary.

endever* corbin, thank you for providing invaluable feedback about Caroline and her experiences. This story is much better for your contributions.

Adrianna Cuevas, you are an A+ critique partner. Thanks for providing feedback and motivation on this book and so many others.

Much thanks to Cathleen Barnhart, Taylor Gardner, Remy Lai, Jen Malia, and Meera Trehan for providing valuable feedback at varying stages of this project.

A big thank-you to the PJ Our Way program for your support of my books and the critical work that you do.

Thanks to Daniel Alhadeff for graciously providing help with Ladino.

I feel privileged to have had the opportunity to portray Sephardic Jewish culture, which is so rarely represented in fiction. Ima and her family were written to honor my maternal grandmother, Ray Farhi Ross. Grandma, I love you and I miss you. I hope I was able to do you proud.

As always, my family has been a source of much-needed support. Thanks to Mom, Dad, Grandpa Charlie, and Aunt Edy. You have done a wonderful job cheering me on and doing what you can to promote my books.

Another big thanks to Wynn and Laurie, the world's best in-laws.

This is a story about sisters, and so I have to extend a special thanks to my own sister, Elisheva Pripas. Thank you for reading an early draft and serving as a Judaism consultant. You also helped me to understand #LittleSisterProblems, which was critical in sorting out Caroline's character motivations. You are a true Caroline: my partner-in-crime who is critical to the entire operation.

Thank you to Ari Ne'eman and Ruti Reagan for your friendship and support.

All of my gratitude to the teachers and librarians who have helped my books find readers, even as the world fell apart. Your work is invaluable and deserves more acknowledgment than it receives.

I would like to express my appreciation for the We Need Diverse Books movement. Your advocacy has made it possible for me to make the books that I do.

Finally, thank you to my husband, Neil. Thank you for always being my first and most supportive reader. You have helped me through all of the ups and downs of being a writer, and everything else in this wild world of ours. I'm so glad you're my lockdown partner, co-cat-parent, and everything else.